# *Sharon Kendrick*

# THE UNLIKELY MISTRESS

**LONDON'S MOST
ELIGIBLE PLAYBOYS**

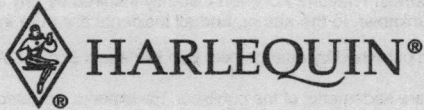

**HARLEQUIN®**

TORONTO • NEW YORK • LONDON
AMSTERDAM • PARIS • SYDNEY • HAMBURG
STOCKHOLM • ATHENS • TOKYO • MILAN • MADRID
PRAGUE • WARSAW • BUDAPEST • AUCKLAND

Caius Niger
For my poet, mentor, muse
and Blue-Eyed Boy.

ISBN 0-373-12227-6

THE UNLIKELY MISTRESS

First North American Publication 2002.

Copyright © 2001 by Sharon Kendrick.

# CHAPTER ONE

SABRINA looked, and then looked again, her heart beating out a guilty beat while she tried to tell herself that her eyes were playing tricks on her. Because he couldn't possibly be for real.

He was standing close to the water, close enough for her to be able to see the carved symmetry of his features. Chiselled cheekbones and a proud, patrician nose. The mouth was luscious—both hard and sensual—a mouth which looked as though it had kissed a lot of women in its time.

Only the eyes stopped the face from being too beautiful—they were too icily cold for perfection. Even from this distance, they seemed to glitter with a vital kind of energy and a black, irresistible kind of danger...

Oh, Lord, thought Sabrina in despair. What am I *thinking* of? She was not the kind of woman to be transfixed by complete strangers—especially not when she was alone and vulnerable in a foreign country. And while Venice was the most beautiful place on earth—she was there on her own.

On her own. Something she was still having to come to term with. Once again, guilt stabbed at her with piercing accuracy.

But still she watched him...

By the edge of the water, Guy felt his body tense with a sense of the unexpected, aware of the unmistakable sensation of being watched. He narrowed hard slate-grey eyes as they scanned the horizon, and his gaze was suddenly arrested by the sight of the woman who drifted in the gondola towards him. Madonna, he thought suddenly. Madonna.

The pale March sun caught a sheen of bright red-gold hair, drifting like a banner around her shoulders. He could see long, slender limbs and skin so pale it looked almost translucent. She's English, he thought suddenly as their eyes clashed across the glittering water. And for one mad, reckless moment he thought about...what? Following her? Buying her a cup of coffee? His mouth hardened into a brief, cynical smile.

It was reckless to want to pick up a total stranger and he, more than most people, knew the folly of being reckless. Hadn't his whole life been spent making amends for his father's one careless act of desperation? The knock-on effect of impulsive behaviour was something to guard against. Resolutely he turned away from her distractions.

Sabrina felt something approaching pain. *Look at me*, she urged him silently, but her gondolier chose that moment to give an expert twist of his wrist to glide the craft into shore and he was lost to her eyes.

She pushed her guidebook back into her handbag and stood up, allowing the gondolier to steady her elbow, nodding her head vigorously, as if she understood every word of his murmured Italian. But she had paid him before the journey and didn't have a clue what he could be saying to her.

And then there was a shout behind her, a deep, alarming shout, and instinctively she knew that the voice belonged to the man with the dark hair. She automatically turned in response, just in time to feel a great whooshing spray of icy cold water as it splashed over her.

It jetted towards her eyes and the shock made her handbag slip from her fingers. She was aware of her gondolier shouting something furiously, and when she opened her eyes again she could see the zigzag of foam left in the wake of a small speedboat.

And the man with the dark hair.

He was standing on the shore right next to her, holding his hand out, and despite the look of icy anger on his face some instinct made her take it, losing herself immediately in the warmth of his firm grasp.

'Why the hell can't people control the machines they're supposed to be in charge of?' he said, in a voice as coolly beautiful as his face. He gave a brief, hard stare at the retreating spray of the boat, then narrowed his eyes as he looked down at the shivering woman whose fingernails were gripping painfully into the palm of his hand. Her face was so white that it looked almost translucent, and he felt a strange kick to his heart. 'You *are* English?'

Up close, he was even more devastating. Breathtakingly so. Awareness shimmered over her skin like fingertips. 'Y-y-yes, I am,' she replied, from between chattering teeth. 'How c-c-could you tell?'

He carried on holding her hand until he was certain that she was grounded. 'Because pale women with freckles and strawberry-blonde hair look quintessentially English, that's why,' he answered slowly as he allowed his eyes to drift irresistibly over her. 'And you're soaking.'

Sabrina looked down at herself, and saw that he wasn't exaggerating. She was wet right through—her T-shirt stained with dirty lagoon water, the pinpoint thrust of her nipples emphasising her plummeting body temperature as much as the chattering of her teeth.

'Not to mention freezing.' He swallowed as he followed the direction of her eyes, tempted to make a flippant joke about wet T-shirt competitions, then deciding against it. Not his scene to make remarks like that to a complete stranger.

Sabrina suddenly realised what was missing. 'Oh, my goodness—I've dropped my handbag!' she wailed.

'Where?'

'In the w-water. And it's got my purse in it!'

He went to peer over the edge of the lagoon, but the dark waters had claimed it.

'Don't!' Sabrina called, terrified that he would just disappear again, exit from her life for ever.

He turned round with a look of mystification. 'Don't what?'

'D-don't t-t-try and retrieve it!'

'You think I'm about to dive into the canal to hunt around for your handbag?' He smiled again. 'Princess, I'm not that much of a hero!' But the smile died on his lips as he saw that the edges of her mouth were turning a very pale blue. 'You know,' he observed slowly, unable to look away from the ice-blue dazzle of her eyes, 'you're really going to have to get out of those wet clothes before you catch pneumonia!'

The intimacy of his remark drove every sane response clean out of her mind. Sabrina opened her mouth, then chattered it shut again.

Guy frowned. He couldn't believe he'd said that. Crass, or what? 'Where are you staying?'

'M-m-miles away.' Naturally. Rooms this close to St Mark's Square tended to be beyond the reach of anyone other than your average millionaire.

Guy's mouth hardened as he read the unconscious appeal in her eyes. Pity she hadn't mentioned that *before* the gondola had sped away. If the driver hadn't been flirting with her quite so outrageously, then he might have been able to warn her about the speedboat in time. And the least he could have done to recompense would have been to give her a free ride back to her hotel.

Which left it up to *him*.

He had achieved what he had set out to do in Venice—had purchased a superb Italian old master for one of his more demanding clients. The price he had bartered had been better than expected and his client would be pleased.

He had planned a quiet day. Playing knight in shining armour hadn't been top of his agenda. But responsibility was etched deep into Guy's personality. He looked down into her heart-shaped face, and felt his heart kick-start again. She really was very beautiful... 'You can't possibly travel home in that state, but you can clean up at my hotel if you like—it's just around the corner.'

'Your *hotel*?' Sabrina swallowed, guiltily remembering the way she had been unable to tear her eyes away from him on the lagoon. She'd been certain that he hadn't seen her—but what if he had? And what if he'd then imagined that she was the kind of woman who allowed herself to be picked up in the most casual manner possible and taken back for a so-called siesta? 'I don't even know you—and I'm not in the habit of going back to strange men's hotel rooms!'

Guy's eyes glittered with unconcealed irritation. He was offering to do her a favour—did she really think that he was after something else? Desperate enough to make a pass at someone he didn't even know?

He supposed that he could have shrugged and said fine and walked away, but something about her defensive stance struck at his conscience. He forced his mouth into a smile. 'Then how about I introduce myself so I'm no longer a stranger?' He held his hand out. 'Guy Masters,' he said softly.

Something in the way he said it struck at Sabrina's heart like a hammer blow, as though she had been waiting all her life to hear just that name spoken aloud. She felt his hand still warming her frozen fingers, his grey eyes sending their icy light across her face, and tiptoes of some unknown emotion began to tingle their way up her spine. 'S-Sabrina Cooper,' she stumbled.

'Well, you'll be quite safe with me, Sabrina Cooper,' he assured her gravely. 'The alternative, of course, is that you travel halfway across Venice looking like that. It's up to you—I'm only offering to help. Take it or leave it.'

His grey eyes didn't stray from her face, which only seemed to reinforce where he *wasn't* looking. And he didn't really want to spell it out. That wet T-shirt did spectacularly draw the eye. Even if the sopping fabric was stretched over a pair of breasts which could in no way be described as voluptuous. On the contrary, he thought, they were small and neat and deliciously cuppable. She wouldn't be *safe* travelling back on her own, looking as beautifully sexy as she did right now.

Sabrina hesitated. Surely a man who looked like Guy Masters would have no need of ulterior motives. 'Why are you being so...?'

'Chivalrous?' he prompted, a cool fire dancing in his eyes. It amused him that she hadn't seen fit to leap at his offer. That didn't happen a lot, not these days. He shrugged. 'Because you're English, and so am I, and I have an over-developed sense of responsibility which just won't seem to go away. You're cold and wet and you've lost your purse. So what else can I do? Rip the clothes from my back in order to cover you up?'

She eyed the taut torso with alarm as her imagination gave her a disturbingly realistic picture of how he would look if he *did* remove that snowy-white T-shirt. What on earth was the matter with her? She had come to Venice in an attempt to make some sense of the tragedy which had transformed her life. And making sense of things did not involve feeling overwhelmingly attracted to men who had a dangerous air of inaccessibility about them.

'Er, no.' She swallowed. 'That won't be necessary. I'll

take up your offer of the bathroom. It's very...sweet of you. Thank you.' But 'sweet' did not seem an appropriate word to use about Guy Masters—he was far too elementally masculine for that.

'Come this way,' he said, and they began to walk through the narrow, dark streets of Venice with the slicking sounds of water all around them.

Sabrina felt the weight of heavy, wet denim chafing uncomfortably against her thighs. 'I don't know how I'm going to get my clothes dry.'

'Don't worry. The hotel will think of something.' Hotels like the Palazzo Regina always did, he thought wryly. Catering for each and every whim of their pampered guests, however bizarre. In life, Guy had realised a long, long time ago, you got what you paid for. And the more you paid, the more impressed the world seemed to be.

Sabrina was aware of the curious looks being cast in their direction, and couldn't decide whether that was because she looked half-drowned or because he looked so beautiful. She felt overpoweringly aware of him as he moved with a kind of restrained power by her side, every pore seeming to exude a vital kind of energy. It was as though that magnificent body had imprinted itself indelibly on every single one of her senses and she could feel the incessant pumping of her heart and the rapid little rush of her breathing as they walked.

'How much money was in your purse?' he asked.

'Only a bit. I've left most of it in my hotel safe, along with my tickets.'

'That's something, I guess. Imagine if you'd come out with your airline tickets.'

'Imagine,' she said faintly.

Something in the way she'd said it made him smile. 'We're here,' he announced, stopping in front of a large, impressive façade overlooking the waterfront itself.

Sabrina screwed her face up in disbelief. 'Here?' He was gorgeous, yes, but in his jeans and T-shirt he had seemed just like her—just another tourist. This couldn't be right, surely? His hotel couldn't be this central—not unless he was staying in some sort of museum or palace. Which was exactly what it looked like. 'You're staying *here*?'

Guy heard the incredulity in her voice and sizzled her a glance of mocking query. 'You think I don't know the way back to my own hotel?'

Sabrina compared it to the tiny, dark *pensione* she was staying in. 'It looks more like a palace than a hotel!'

'Mmm. I believe it was.' He glanced down and saw that the walk had removed that ghastly blue tinge from her lips, and smiled. 'A very long time ago.'

'How long?'

'Fourteenth century, would you believe?'

'Good heavens,' said Sabrina lightly, and the question came out before she had time to think about it. 'How on earth can you afford to stay in a place like this?'

Years of self-preservation against women with dollar signs in their eyes made Guy reply, without missing a beat, 'I'm lucky,' he said coolly. 'The company pays for it. Come on. You've started shivering again.'

As soon as they walked into a lavishly ornate foyer, she heard the faint buzz of comment. One of the men working at the reception desk, who looked handsome enough to be a movie star, fixed Guy Masters with an unctuous smile.

'Sir? I trust you have had an enjoyable morning.'

'Eventful,' Guy murmured. 'I'll just have my key, please, Luigi.'

'Certainly, sir, I'll have someone—'

'No, please, don't bother. I'll see myself up.'

In the mirror-lined lift, Sabrina saw how wet she really was.

The water of the lagoon was obviously much dirtier than

its colour suggested, because there were tiny spots of mud spattering her T-shirt. And unfortunately there were two damp circles ringing her breasts, drawing attention to the outline of her bra which was embarrassingly visible. And so, too, were her nipples, tight and hot and aching. Turned on by a man she had only just met...

Appalled by her dark and unwanted thoughts, she quickly crossed her arms and clamped them over her bust. 'That man at Reception gave me a very funny look.'

Guy felt a pulse flicker as he stared at her reflection in the mirror, noting the protective body language and working out for himself the reason for it. 'Well, you must admit you do look pretty spectacular,' he murmured. Like some glorious nymph who had just emerged from the water.

'Mmmm,' she agreed. 'Spectacularly drowned.'

He narrowed his eyes. Her voice was unusually soft. As soft as her lips. The lift pinged to a halt. 'Here's my suite.'

*Suite?*

Sabrina thought of her own small *pensione*, where she could never find anyone on duty. Like last night, for example, when the water coming from the tap had been nothing more than a dark, brackish trickle. With the aid of her phrasebook, she had been forced to laboriously construct a note to the *manager*, requesting that he do something about the hot water. What if she'd gone back today, dripping from head to toe in filthy lagoon water, to discover that nothing had been resolved?

Thank heavens for the chivalrous Guy Masters, she told herself—but she felt a mixture of nerves and excitement as he unlocked the door to his suite.

He pushed open the door to let her inside and Sabrina had to stifle a small cry of astonishment as she walked into a high-ceilinged sitting room. Because, yes, of course, she'd known that places such as these existed, but it was something so outside her own experience that it was like stepping into a parallel world.

The room was full of furniture which even an idiot could tell was very old. Antique, in fact. And priceless too, she imagined.

Sabrina looked around her. The light was muted because all the shutters were closed, but that made the contents of the room stand out even more.

Silken rugs in jewel-bright colours were scattered on the marble floors, on which stood spindly-legged chairs and tables. There was a faded sofa of crimson and gold and a couple of chairs which matched, all strewn with cushions of the same rich colours. She slowly turned to see an oil painting of a long-dead doge, set against the timeless Venetian backdrop, one of many paintings hung on the crimson walls.

'Oh, but it's beautiful,' she breathed. 'So beautiful.'

Guy watched her slow appraisal, her uninhibited pleasure making her look curiously elegant, despite the damp and dirty clothes.

'Isn't it?' he said softly, but he wasn't even looking at the painting.

And the lack of light was far too intimate, he decided suddenly, striding over to the window to push open the shutters, so the reflected light from the Grand Canal gleamed and glittered back into the room at them.

A view like that was worth a king's ransom, thought Sabrina, suddenly feeling as out of place as some scruffy urchin who had come seeking shelter from the storm.

It brought her quickly to her senses. She wasn't here to enjoy the view. Or to make small-talk. She had better just clean up and be on her way.

She cleared her throat. 'Could you show me—?'

He turned around, noting the sudden pinkness in her cheeks, the two high spots of colour making her look like some flaxen-plaited doll. 'Sure. The bathroom's that door over there.' He pointed. 'Take as long as you like. Oh, and throw your wet clothes out and I'll send them down and have them laundered.'

'Thank you.'

Sabrina was glad to lock the bathroom door behind her and peel off the freezing clothes from her shivering flesh. They smelt so *dank*!

The jeans were first, and then the T-shirt, and she dropped the sodden garments onto the marble floor. But her bra and panties were damp with canal water, too. Should she risk…?

Risk what? she asked herself impatiently. She couldn't keep sodden underwear on, and this pair of sensible cotton briefs was hardly likely to have him trying to beat the door down!

Sheltering behind the screen of the door, she picked the bundle up.

'Guy?'

'Leave them outside,' came a muffled sort of voice, and she did as he asked, quickly slamming the door shut and sliding the lock home before stepping into the shower, with its industrial-sized head.

Outside, Guy gingerly picked up the deposited items as if he were handling a poisonous snake.

Had it really been necessary for her to take *everything* off? he wondered uncomfortably, while asking himself why some women chose to wear knickers which looked as if they were armour-plated.

He knew almost nothing about Sabrina Cooper, and would never see her again after today, but what he *did* know was that she certainly hadn't come to Venice with seduction in mind.

Not unless she was intending to appeal to the type of man who got turned on by the frumpy gym-mistress look!

Biting back a smile, he wandered over to the telephone and picked up the receiver.

'*Pronto!*' he drawled for courtesy's sake, and then immediately switched to English, in which most of the staff were fluent. His Italian was passable—but in a case concerning a strange woman's underwear he needed no misunderstandings! 'How long will it take to get some clothes laundered?'

There was a short pause. 'Certainly within a couple of hours, sir.'

Guy frowned. That long? And just what were they supposed to do while Sabrina's jeans and T-shirt and bra and panties whizzed around in the washing machine? His time was precious, and his leisure time especially so. There were a million things he would rather be doing than being forced to sit and chat to someone with whom he had nothing in common other than that they both hailed from the same country.

*Damn!*

'Let's try for half that time, shall we?' he suggested softly. 'And can you have some coffee brought up at the same time?'

Bearing a tray of coffee, the valet came and collected the damp garments and Guy heard the sound of the shower being turned off. He walked over to the bathroom door.

'I'm afraid your clothes won't be back for an hour,' he called.

'An *hour*?' Sabrina's heart plummeted as she stood behind the locked door. What was she supposed to do in the meantime? Stay wrapped in a towel inside this steamy bathroom?

He heard the annoyance in her voice and felt like telling her that the idea pleased him even less than it did her. But he hadn't been forced to bring her back here, had he? No, he'd made that decision all on his own—so he could hardly complain about it now.

'Why don't you use that towelling robe hanging up on the back of the door?' he suggested evenly. 'And there's some coffee out here when you're ready.'

Squinting at herself in the cloudy mirror, Sabrina shrugged on a towelling gown which was as luxuriously thick and fluffy as she would expect in a place like this. She slipped it over her bare, freckled shoulders, and as she did so she became aware of the faint trace of male scent which clung to it.

Guy had been wearing this robe before her, she realised as an unwelcome burst of sexual hunger grew into life inside her. Guy's body had been as naked beneath this as her own now was. She felt the sudden picking up of her heart as the evocative muskiness invaded her nostrils, and she wondered if she might be going slightly mad.

How could a complete stranger—however attractive he undoubtedly was—manage to have such an incapacitating and powerful effect on her? Making her feel like some puppet jerked and manipulated by invisible strings. Was this what the death of her fiancé had turned her into—some kind of predator?

Guy glanced up as she walked in and his grey eyes narrowed, a pulse hammering at his temple. Maybe the robe hadn't been such a good idea after all, he conceded. Because wasn't there something awfully erotic about a woman wearing an oversized masculine garment like that? On him it reached to just below his knees—but on this woman's pale and slender frame it almost skimmed her ankles.

'How about some coffee?' he queried steadily.

'C-coffee would be lovely,' she stumbled, suddenly feeling acutely shy. She perched on the edge of a sofa on the opposite side of the room, telling herself that she had absolutely nothing to worry about. The circumstances might be bizarre, but for some reason she trusted this man. Men of Guy Masters's calibre wouldn't make a clumsy pass at a stranger, despite that brief, hungry darkening of his eyes.

He poured them both coffee and thought that conversation might be safer than silence. 'First time in Venice?'

'First time abroad,' she admitted.

'You're kidding!'

She shook her head. 'No, I'm not. I've never been out of England before.' Michael hadn't earned very much, and neither had she—and saving up to buy a house had seemed more important than trips abroad. Though a man like Guy Masters would probably not understand that.

'And you came here on your own?'

'That's right.'

He looked at her curiously. 'Pretty daring thing to do,' he observed, 'first time in a foreign country on your own?'

Sabrina stared down at the fingers which were laced around her coffee-cup. 'I've never done anything remotely daring before...'

'What, never?' he teased softly.

Sabrina didn't smile back. Hadn't she decided that life was too short to play safe all the time? 'So I thought I'd give it a try,' she said solemnly, and shifted her bottom back a little further on the seat.

Guy sipped his coffee and wished that she would sit still, not keep shifting around on the sofa as if she had ants in her pants. And then he remembered.

*She wasn't wearing any.*

Dear God. A shaft of desire shot through him, which was as unexpected as it was inappropriate, and he took a huge mouthful of coffee—almost glad when it scalded his lips. He risked a surreptitious glance at his watch. Only forty-five minutes to go. Less if he was lucky. Much more of this and he would be unable to move.

'So why Venice?' he queried, a slight edge of desperation to his voice.

'Oh, it's one of the world's most beautiful cities, and I—I had to...to...'

Something in the quality of her hesitation made him stir with interest. 'Had to what?'

She had been about to say 'get away', but that particular statement always provoked the questions to ask why, and once that question had been asked then the whole sad story would come out. A story she was weary of telling. Weary of living through. She had come to Italy to escape from death and its clutches.

'I had to see St Mark's Square.' She smiled brightly. 'It was something of a life's ambition. So was riding in a gondola.'

'But not taking a bath in the Grand Canal?'

She actually laughed. 'No. Not that. I hadn't bargained on that!'

He thought how the laugh lit up her face. Like sunshine glowing from within. 'And how long are you staying?'

'Only a couple more days. How about you?'

He felt a pulse begin to beat insistently at his temple. Suddenly Venice was getting more attractive by the minute—rather uncomfortably attractive, actually. 'Me, too,' he said huskily, and risked another glance at his watch.

The room seemed much too small. Much too intimate. Again Sabrina shifted self-consciously on the sofa.

'How old are you?' he demanded suddenly, as she crossed one pale, slender thigh over the other.

Old enough to recognise that maybe Guy Masters wasn't completely indifferent to her after all. The quiet, metallic gleam in the cool grey eyes told her that. But that wasn't the kind of answer he was seeking.

'I'm twenty-seven,' she told him.

'You look younger.'

'So people say.' She lifted her eyebrows. 'And you?'

'Thirty-two.'

'You look older.'

Their eyes connected as something primitive shuddered in the air around them.

'I know I do,' he murmured.

His words caressed her and Sabrina stared at him, unable to stop her eyes from committing every exquisite feature to memory. I will never forget you, she thought with an aching sense of sadness. Ever.

They sat in silence for a while as they drank their coffee. Eventually, there was a rap on the door and the valet delivered an exquisitely laundered set of underwear, jeans and T-shirt. Guy handed them over to her. 'There you go,' he said gravely.

She took them, blushingly aware that his fingertips had actually been touching the pressed cotton of her bra and panties. 'I'd better go and get changed.'

And if he'd thought that she'd looked exquisite before, that was nothing to the transformation which had taken place when she emerged, shimmering, from the bathroom. Guy didn't know what the laundry had managed to do with her clothes, but they now looked as if they were brand-new, and her hair had dried to a glorious strawberry-blonde sheen which spilled over her shoulders.

'You'd better take this,' he said as he dug deep into the pocket of his trousers and withdrew a wad of money, seeing her eyes widen in an alarmed question as he gave it to her.

'What's this?' she demanded.

'Didn't you drop your purse into the water?' he queried softly. 'And don't you need to get home?'

'I can't take your money,' she protested.

'Then don't. Think of it as a loan. Pay me back tomorrow if you like.'

Sabrina slid the notes thoughtfully into the back pocket of her jeans. 'OK. I will. Thanks.'

He went down with her in the lift to the foyer, telling himself that he would never see her again.

And wondering why that thought should make him ache so much, and so badly.

# CHAPTER TWO

DESPITE telling herself that she was being crazy and unrealistic, Sabrina couldn't help the decided spring to her step next morning as she set off to return Guy's money, nor the flush of anticipation which made her cheeks glow. And why had she dressed up for him in an ice-blue sundress which very nearly matched her eyes and peep-toed sandals which made her legs look longer than they really were?

Surely she didn't imagine for a moment that he would take one look at her and decide that she was the woman of his dreams?

She put the stack of lire in an envelope. He probably wouldn't even be there, she reasoned. She would just have to leave the money for him at Reception.

The buildings soared up all around her and the water—which was everywhere—seemed to glimmer and glitter with some unspoken promise. As her steps drew her closer to Guy's hotel, she felt the slow prickle of nerves.

She told herself that even if he was there he would probably just take the money with that cool, enigmatic smile and thank her. Then say goodbye, his faintly quizzical expression mocking her if she was foolish enough to linger hopefully over their farewells.

Drawing a deep breath, she walked into the foyer, surprised that the man behind the desk with the movie-star looks should raise his eyebrows in recognition the moment he saw her. He quickly picked up the telephone and started speaking into it.

By the time she had reached the desk he had finished his

call and was glancing down at a notepad in front of him. He smiled at her.

'Ah, Signorina Cooper,' he purred.

She raised her eyebrows. 'You know my name?'

The smile widened. 'But of course! Signor Masters asked me to telephone him the moment you arrived.'

Well, that was something. At least he hadn't imagined that she'd just disappeared into the sunset with his money.

She quickly took the envelope from her handbag. 'Can I just leave this here for him?' she said breathlessly. 'I won't stay. I'm—'

'Not planning on running away from me, are you, Miss Cooper?' came a deep voice from just behind her, and Sabrina turned round to find herself caught in the hard, grey crossfire of his eyes. And she was lost. Utterly lost.

'Hello, Guy,' she said weakly.

'Hello, Sabrina,' he mocked, his gaze running over her with pleasure, thinking that she had dressed up for him, and the rapid beat of his heart told him exactly what *that* meant.

'I brought your money back.' She held the envelope out.

'So I see.'

'I can't thank you enough for coming to my rescue. I don't know how I would have managed otherwise.' She swallowed down the constricting lump which was affecting her ability to breathe. 'Anyway, I'd better go—'

But he cut her words short with the restraining touch of his fingertips on her bare arm—a feather-light and innocent enough touch, but one which made sensation skate erotic little whispers all over its surface. He felt suddenly breathless. *Reckless.*

His eyes darkened. 'Why go anywhere?' he questioned softly. It's a beautiful day. We're both on our own. Why don't we go sightseeing together?'

'Together?'

He paused for a dangerous beat, giving her the unthinkable opportunity of saying no. 'Unless you'd rather be on your own?'

Well, that was why she had come to Venice, wasn't it? To get away and escape. To throw off the shackles of anxious eyes which followed her every move.

But Sabrina didn't want to get away. Not from Guy. She tried to keep her voice casual. 'Not especially.'

Guy almost laughed aloud at her lukewarm response. He wondered if she did this all the time—sent out these conflicting messages so that while that flushed look of anticipation and the bright sparkle of her eyes were like a sweet invitation to possess her, the somewhat indifferent responses to his questions were a slammed door in the face. Perplexing. And he hadn't been perplexed by a woman in a long time.

'So is that a yes or a no?'

It was an I'm-not-sure-whether-I'm-doing-the-right-thing, Sabrina thought, but she smiled anyway. 'It's a yes,' she said.

He watched the way she flicked her hair back over her shoulder. The movement made her breasts dance beneath the thin cotton dress, and Guy felt the primitive urge to take her somewhere and impale her and make her his. He hardened his mouth, appalled at himself.

'Why don't you tell me what you've seen already?' he suggested unevenly. 'And where you'd like to eat lunch?'

Sabrina noticed the sudden tension around his mouth, the way his eyes had darkened into a hungry glitter, and while she knew that she ought to be intimidated by the sheer potency of his masculinity she had never felt less intimidated in her life.

'I've seen the Basilica di San Marco,' she said. 'Of course! And the Golden House and the Doges Palace. But that's all. Lunch—I wouldn't have a clue about.' Her budget was tight and she'd been skipping lunch. But that had been no hardship.

Guy noticed the shadowed hollows beneath the high sweep of her cheekbones and wondered if she had been eating properly. 'Then let's go and find the rest of Venice,' he suggested softly.

But it took an effort for Sabrina to concentrate on her surroundings as they walked out into the sunshine. Yesterday the city had seemed like the most magical place on the planet, while today it was difficult to think about anything other than the man at her side.

At least she had some idea of what she was supposed to be looking at. She'd spent the preceding weeks reading every book about Venice that she could lay her hands on—it had been a good kind of displacement therapy—but Guy could more than match her.

'Did you know that the humorist Robert Benchley sent a telegram when he arrived in Venice?' Guy murmured. 'Saying, "Streets full of water. Please advise."'

Sabrina thought that his grey eyes looked soft, soft as the cream silk shirt he wore. 'No, I didn't know that. But Truman Capote said that Venice was like eating an entire box of chocolate liqueurs in one go.'

'Oh, did he?' He liked the quickness of her mind, the way her thoughts matched his own. Liked the fact that she'd researched the place so thoroughly. He felt his heart begin to pick up its beat as he stared down at her, at the strawberry-blonde hair which gleamed like bright gold in the midday sun and the slim, pale column of her neck. There was a fragility about her which was rare in a modern woman, he thought, and wondered what it would be like to take her in his arms. Take her to his bed. Whether she would bend or break...

He realised that they had spent the best part of two hours together and she hadn't asked him a single question about his life back in England. And he noticed that she'd been quietly evasive on the subject of her own life.

But why not? he thought with a sudden sense of liberation. Wasn't anonymity a kind of freedom in itself? Didn't he live the kind of life where people judged him before they had even met him, depending on what they'd heard about him?

The bell of San Marco rang out twice, and Guy looked at his watch. 'We'd better try and find a table for lunch while there's still time.'

Sabrina stared up into dark grey eyes and felt her skin prickle in heated reaction. 'I'm not hungry.'

'Is that why you're so thin?' he demanded. 'Because you skip lunch?'

'Thanks very much!'

'Oh, I'm not complaining,' he murmured, as his eyes drifted over her. 'Your cheekbones are quite exquisitely pronounced and your legs are just the right side of slender. I suppose you have to work at it, the same as every other woman.'

Sabrina let her gaze fall from his face, staring instead at the pink-tipped toes which peeped through her strappy sandals, remembering how she'd forced herself to paint them, telling herself that out of such small, unimportant rituals some kind of normal life would be resumed.

'Sabrina,' he said softly. 'What's the matter? It was supposed to be a compliment. Have I insulted you? Embarrassed you?'

She looked up again. Now would be the perfect time to tell him that the weight had simply fallen away after Michael's death. But tell him that and she would be back playing the unwanted role of the bereaved fiancée. Was it selfish of her to want to play a different part? To want to feel the sun warm and alive on her cheeks and see the unmistakable glint of appreciation in the eyes of the man who stood looking down at her? To feel *alive* again, instead of half-dead herself?

She shook herself out of her reverie and forced a smile which, to her suprise, felt as if it wanted to stay on her mouth. 'By telling me I'm thin? Come on, Guy—did you ever hear of a woman who was offended by that?'

Her smile was like the sun nudging out from behind a cloud, he thought. 'I guess not.' Come to think of it, he didn't have much appetite himself, and certainly not for conventional fare.

Instead, he found himself wondering how her lips would taste and what the scent of her breath would be like against his. He shook his head to dispel the sensual imagery. 'Why don't we have coffee and a pastry at one of these cafés in the square?' he suggested steadily. 'It's warm enough to sit outside in the sunshine.'

They found a vacant table and ordered pastries with their coffee, the lightest and most beautiful cakes imaginable, and Guy thought that they tasted like sawdust in his mouth. And saw that Sabrina had taken exactly two mouthfuls herself.

'It must be the heat.' She shrugged in response to the mocking question in his eyes.

'So it must.' He echoed the lie, knowing that their lack of hunger had nothing to do with the temperature.

He marched her through the city like a professional tour guide, as if determined that he should show her everything. Sabrina wondered what had provoked this sudden, relentless pace, but she was too bewitched by him to care.

They stood side by side on the Bridge of Sighs and stared into the dark waters beneath.

'Look down there,' said Sabrina suddenly. 'And think of the thousands of tourists who have stood here like this and been affected by this amazing city.'

His heart missed a beat as enchantment washed over him. 'You mean the way it's affecting us now?'

'Yes.' She told herself it wasn't *that* remarkable for him to have echoed her thoughts, but still her voice trembled. 'That's exactly what I mean.'

He wanted her, he thought. And she wanted him. 'Are you going to have dinner with me tonight, Sabrina?' he asked suddenly.

She didn't even stop to think about it, or bother to wonder whether she'd made it too easy for him. 'You know I am.'

He nodded, the thrill of anticipation making his heart pick up speed. 'Tell me where you're staying and I'll pick you up at eight.'

'You don't have to do that.'

Her reluctance sharpened an appetite already keenly honed. 'Oh, but I insist,' he contradicted softly.

But pride made her match his determination. He must be some kind of hot-shot to be staying at that hotel. She didn't want him seeing her humble little *pensione*, emphasising how great the differences between them. Just now they were as close to equal as they would ever be and she wanted to hold onto that. 'I'll meet you in the square. Honestly, Guy, I'm an independent woman, you know!'

'Well, sometimes a man doesn't want an independent woman,' he ground out. He couldn't believe he'd just said that, but he had. Or that he'd caught her by the arm to feel the soft tremble of flesh where his fingers burnt so delectably against her bare skin. 'Are you always this damned stubborn?'

Something in the heated frustration of his question made Sabrina's blood sing with a glorious inevitability, and she had the sense of being led towards something which defied all logic. It was liberation at its most intense and powerful, and she was no longer heartbroken, bereaved Sabrina. For one enchanted moment she stood poised on the brink of something magical.

She smiled. 'Only if I need to be.'

There was a long and dangerous pause. 'But I'm used to getting my own way,' he told her steadily.

'I know you are. It shows.'

She looked down at his tanned fingers which still lay against her white skin, and he let his hand fall, perplexed by his own actions. He was a man whose reputation hinged on being in control—so why was he acting as if he were auditioning for the leading role in a Western movie?

'Was I being unbearably high-handed?' he asked her, missing the satin feel of her skin beneath his fingertips.

She took one last look at him as she stepped into the water-taxi which had slid to a halt beside them. Not unbearably anything, she thought. You wouldn't know how to be. 'Only a little.' She shrugged. 'I'll see you tonight at eight.'

And Guy was left staring at the back of her bright blonde head, his heart thundering with a mixture of admiration and frustration.

# CHAPTER THREE

Sabrina was twenty minutes late. Guy had never had a woman keep him waiting in his life and he couldn't decide whether to be irritated or intrigued. He glanced down at his watch for the umpteenth time and actually began to wonder whether he'd been stood up.

But then he saw her crossing the square, wearing some slinky little silver-grey dress with a filmy silver stole around her pale shoulders, her legs looking deliciously long in spindly, high-heeled shoes.

Sabrina spotted his tall, brooding figure straight away, as if he had been programmed to dominate her whole horizon. He was wearing a pale grey unstructured suit which did nothing to disguise the hard, muscular body beneath. And, outwardly at least, he looked completely relaxed, but as she grew closer she could see a coiled kind of tension, which gave him the dark, irresistible shimmer of danger. He looked completely relaxed, but there was no mistaking the watchful quality which made his grey eyes gleam with sub-dued promise.

She had very nearly not come tonight, lifting the telephone to ring Guy's hotel more than once, telling herself that this was fast turning into something she hadn't planned. Something she wasn't sure if she could handle.

Or stop.

But something had prevented her cancelling—something she couldn't quite put her finger on. Maybe it was the memory of that first, glorious sight of him. Leaving behind the knowledge that if she were never to see him again, then the world would never seem quite the same place.

His smile widened as she approached, but he made no move towards her. Let her come to me, he thought. He wanted to watch the way she moved—her hips unconsciously thrusting forward, the fluid sway of her bottom. He imagined those hips crushed beneath the hard contours of his own, and swallowed. *Come to me, baby*, he thought silently. *Come.*

'Hello,' Sabrina said breathlessly, but something in the darkening of his eyes seemed to have robbed her of the ability to suck air into her lungs.

'Hello.' So. No blurted little excuses for being late. No shrugged or coy reasons. Her carelessness sharpened his desire for her even more intensely and he felt his senses clamour into life. 'Where would you like to eat?'

There was a new, dangerous quality about Guy tonight, Sabrina thought. A danger which should have frightened her, but instead filled her with a sense of almost unendurable excitement. And inevitability. 'You know the city far better than I do,' she said huskily. 'You choose.'

'OK,' he said easily, and for a moment felt the penitent shimmer of guilt. As if he hadn't just spent an hour under the hammering power of the shower, deciding exactly where he wanted to take her. He had opened his mouth to the torrent of water which had beaten down on him, his body growing hard with frustration as he remembered that Sabrina had stood naked beneath these same icy jets.

Except that he doubted whether *she* had needed an ice-cold shower to ward off a desire which was stronger than any desire he could remember.

The restaurant was close by and its menu was famous. It was private and discreet but not in the least bit stuffy; he wondered whether she would comment on its proximity to his hotel, but she didn't.

And it wasn't until they were seated in the darkened alcove he had expressly requested that he relaxed enough to expel a long, relieved breath. She was here, he thought exultantly. Sabrina was *here*. Her hair was all caught back in a smooth pleat at the back of her head and he wanted to reach out and tumble it all the way down her back.

'You look beautiful,' he said slowly.

The way he was looking at her made her feel beautiful. She savoured the compliment, held onto it and tried it out in her mind. 'Why, thank you,' she said demurely.

'I thought you weren't coming.' He couldn't believe he'd just said that either. Hadn't the hard lessons of his childhood meant that he'd spent his whole life striving for some kind of invulnerability?

'I nearly didn't.' Oh, God, she thought, please don't ask me why. Because I might just have to tell you that I knew, if I came, where I might end up spending the night.

'What changed your mind?'

'I was hungry.'

He laughed as the waiter came over with the menus, and Sabrina took hers with hands which had begun to tremble. She wondered whether Guy had noticed.

He had. But he hadn't needed to see her fingers shaking to know that she was working herself up to a fever pitch of sexual excitement which almost matched his own. That was evident enough from the soft line of colour which suffused the high curve of her cheekbones and the hectic glitter of her eyes. The way her lips looked all swollen and pouting, parting moistly of their own volition, the rosy pink tip of her tongue peeping through. And the way the buds of her tiny breasts pushed like metal studs against the silvery silk of her gown.

His grey eyes glittered into hers as she stared unseeingly at the menu. 'Want me to order for you?'

Strange she should be so grateful for a question which would normally have left her open-mouthed with indignation. 'Yes, please.'

His eyes scanned the menu uninterestedly. About the only things he felt like eating right now were oysters, followed by a great big dish of dark, juicy cherries—and it didn't take a great stretch of the imagination to work out why that was.

Guy shifted his chair a little, relieved that the heavy white damask of the tablecloth concealed the first heavy throbbing of desire. Another first, he thought wryly, unable to remember a time when he'd been so exquisitely aroused by a woman without any touch being involved.

He ordered *Brodetto di pesce* followed by *moleche*. Dessert he would take an option on. He had his own ideas for dessert...

The waiter brought over a bottle of the bone-dry Breganze *bianco*, but Sabrina felt intoxicated just by the lazy promise of his smile.

'I don't know if I need any wine,' she admitted.

'Me neither.' He shrugged, but he poured them half a glass each and signalled for some water.

Sabrina sipped at her drink, feeling suddenly shy, not daring to look up, afraid of what she would see in the grey dazzle of his eyes. Or what he might read in hers...

'You know, we've spent nearly the whole day together— and I don't know a single thing about you,' he observed softly. 'I'm not used to women being quite so mysterious.'

Sabrina put her glass down. Here it came. The getting-to-know-you talk. A talk she most emphatically did not want to have. She'd been touched by a tragedy which had left her tainted, simply by association. People treated you differently once they found out and she didn't want Guy to treat her differently. She wanted him to carry on exactly as he was.

She forced a lightness into her voice. 'What exactly do you want to know?'

Guy narrowed his eyes. Women usually loved talking

about themselves. Give them an opener like that and you couldn't shut them up for hours. 'It isn't supposed to be an interrogation session,' he informed her softly, and then he leaned across the table, dark mischief dancing in his eyes. 'Why? Have you got some dark, guilty secret you're keeping from me, Sabrina? Don't tell me—in real life you're a lap-dancer?'

His outrageous question lifted some of the tension, and Sabrina found herself smiling back. 'Much more exciting than that! I work in a bookshop, actually,' she confided, and waited for his reaction.

'A bookshop?' he repeated slowly.

'That's right.' Now it was her turn for mischief. 'You know. They sell those things consisting of pages glued together along one side and bound—'

'And why,' he said, with a smile playing at the corners of his lips, 'do you work in a bookshop?'

She took a sip of her wine. 'Oh, all the usual reasons— I love books. I'm a romantic. I have a great desire to exist on low wages. Do you want me to go on?'

'All night,' he murmured. 'All night.' But then their fish soup arrived and Guy stared at his darkly, wishing that he had known her longer. Wishing that she was already his lover so that he could have suggested that they leave the food untouched and just go straight home to bed. 'And where exactly is this bookshop?'

Sabrina nibbled at a piece of bread. 'In Salisbury. Right next to the Cathedral. Do you know it?'

'Nope. I've never been there,' he said thoughtfully.

She studied the curved dip at the centre of his upper lip and shamelessly found herself wanting to run her tongue along its perfect outline. 'How about you? Where do you live? What kind of work do you do?' She thought of the man she had first seen, in jeans and T-shirt. 'It must be something pretty high-powered for your company to pay for a hotel like that.'

Guy hesitated. When people said that money talked, they didn't realise that it also swore. It sounded ridiculous to consider yourself as being *too* highly paid, but he'd long ago realised that wealth had drawbacks all of its own. And when you were deemed rich—in a world where money was worshipped more than any of the more traditional gods—then lots of people wanted to know you for all the wrong reasons.

Not that he would have put Sabrina into that category. But he liked the sweet, unaffected way she was with him. He hadn't been treated as an equal for a very long time. And if he started hinting at just how much he was really worth, might she not be slightly overawed?

'Oh, I'm just a wheeler-dealer,' he shrugged.

'And what does a wheeler-dealer do?'

He smiled. 'A bit of everything. I buy and sell. Property. Art. Sometimes even cars. Houses occasionally.' But there was no disguising the dismissiveness in his voice as he topped her wine up. 'All pretty boring stuff. Finish your soup.'

'I have finished.'

She'd barely touched it, he noticed as the waiter removed their plates—but, then, neither had he. And he was still aroused. So aroused that...

Sabrina saw the dark colour which had flared over his cheekbones and suddenly she felt weak. Across the table they stared at one another, and the sounds of the other diners retreated so that they might have been alone in the crowded room.

'G-Guy,' she stumbled, through the ragged movement of her breathing.

'What is it?' he murmured.

'The waiter is w-waiting to give us our main course.'

Guy looked up to find the waiter standing beside the table, holding two plates containing crayfish and barely able to contain his smile.

'*Grazie,*' said Guy tightly.

'*Prego.*' The waiter grinned.

Sabrina smoothed her fingers over her flushed cheeks. She didn't speak until the waiter was out of earshot. 'Did you see his face?' she whispered.

'We're in Italy,' he remarked, with a shrug. 'They're used to couples displaying...' he lingered over a wholly inappropriate word '...affection. Now eat your crayfish,' he urged softly.

Like two condemned prisoners eating a last meal, they both silently spooned the crayfish into their mouths. It was fine food, meant to be savoured and enjoyed, but they both ate it quickly, without tasting it. In fact, Guy only just refrained from shovelling it down as if he were on a ten-minute lunch-break.

Sabrina wondered why she didn't feel shy. Or embarrassed. Why being with Guy in an atmosphere so tense with expectation seemed to feel so right. Something she needed more than anything in the world. She put her knife and fork down with a shaky hand and saw that Guy had mirrored her movements.

'Shall I call for the bill?' he queried.

She forced herself to try and respond normally, even though she knew what he meant by his question. 'Don't you want dessert? Or coffee?'

His mouth curved. He heard the delicious thunder of the inevitable. 'I thought we could try somewhere else for coffee.'

'Yes,' she agreed with nervous excitement, because she knew exactly what he meant—and wouldn't a well-brought up girl be frightened by that? Or outraged? 'I guess we could.'

In a daze she allowed him to drape the wrap around her shoulders, feeling the negligent brush of his fingertips against her bare flesh as he did so, and she felt the breath catch in her throat like dust.

He took her by the hand and led her outside into the starry night, looking down at her with soft, silver light gleaming from his eyes.

'You're shivering,' he observed quietly, tracing a thoughtful fingertip down the slim, pale column of her neck and seeing her tremble even more. 'Again.'

'Y-yes.'

He took his jacket off and draped it around her shoulders; the broad cut of it almost swamped her slender frame. 'Here, take this...'

'You'll get cold yourself,' she objected.

'I don't think there's any danger of that,' he said softly, and, sliding his arms around her waist, he bent his head to kiss her.

Her heart was blazing as her mouth parted to meet the first sweet touch of his lips. She ignored the half-hearted voice of her conscience telling her to stop this, because who could have stopped *this*?

He was breathing life into her, bringing warmth flooding back into her veins. As though she had been some cold, bloodless statue and now...now...

'Oh, Guy,' she whispered, in a distracted plea. 'Guy.' But the words were lost against the honeyed softness of his mouth.

Desire shafted through him like an arrow. 'Oh, God, yes, Sabrina,' he ground out, on a sultry note of hunger. 'Yes, and yes, and yes.' He brought her closer into his body, up to the cradle of his hips, where the hard, lean power of him was unmistakable. And now it was Guy's turn to make a harsh little sound. He broke the kiss off with a supreme effort, tearing his mouth away to look down with frustrated perplexity into her disappointed eyes.

'This is all threatening to get out of hand,' he groaned, sucking in a shuddering breath which scorched the lining of his lungs. 'I haven't engaged in such a public display of passion for a long time.' He had always liked beds—clean sheets and clinical comfort—so why was he having to swallow down the primitive urge to lead her to the nearest narrow, dark alleyway, pin her up against some ancient wall and do it to her right there...?

She felt no fear, and no shame. Only an overwhelming need to be near him. She trickled a questing fingertip down the proud, hard lines of his face. 'M-me neither.'

He forced himself to bite out the question, even though it was the most difficult thing he had ever had to say. 'Do you want me to take you back to your hotel, or would you like to...?' The word trailed off temptingly.

'To what?' she asked softly.

'To come back with me? We could have that dessert. Coffee. What do you think? Would you like that, princess?'

'Yes,' she whispered, knowing that he didn't want coffee any more than she did.

He took her hand and led her through the darkened streets. She felt dizzy with the sense of his proximity but she was so disorientated that he could have been leading her to the ends of the earth for all she knew. Or cared.

It wasn't until they found themselves back in the grand elegance of his suite, with the hazy gleam of the lamps falling like moonlight on her flushed cheeks, that something of the enormity of what she was about to embark on began to seep into Sabrina's consciousness. She ought to stop this, she told herself, and stop it right now.

Yet the longer she stared into the mesmerising glitter of those dark-lashed eyes, the harder it was to listen to reason.

Because reason was a weak component in the presence of raw need.

And Michael had taught her that nothing was certain. His death had brought the frailty of life crashing home in a way that nothing else could have done. Why, she could walk out of this room right now and something could happen to ensure that she would never see Guy Masters again. And never know the warmth of his embrace, or taste the luxury of his kiss.

She turned her face up to his, but her half-felt protest became a moan of surrender as he drove his mouth down on hers with a hungry kiss which splintered her senses.

He reached out to remove the clip from her hair, murmured his warm pleasure as it fell in a red-blonde gleam around her shoulders. 'See how your hair glows like fire against your skin. And how your eyes sparkle like pure, clear aquamarines.'

She had never been seduced by words before, had never known their sweet, wanton power. 'G-Guy,' she said shakily.

His eyes gleamed like silver and onyx. 'I want to see you, to see your flesh glow in the moonlight. I want to undress you.' He moved his hand distractedly to find the zip of her dress, before sliding it down with unsteady fingers, kissing her neck as the silky material parted for him.

She gasped as she felt the touch of his fingers against her burning skin and the weight of his hands as they moved down to possessively cup the curve of her bottom. Her head fell helplessly against his shoulder as she felt her dress begin to slide down over her thighs.

'God, princess, you're driving me *crazy*,' he ground out on a shudder as the dress pooled with a silken whisper at her feet. He lifted his head to gaze at her, taken aback by the sight of her frivolous underwear.

It was the last thing he had been expecting—she looked

like a centrefold. A pure white lace bra through which her
nipples peaked rosy and hard, and a matching wisp of a
G-string through which he could distinctly see the red-gold
blur of hair. And then there was the outrageous little sus-
pender belt, onto which were clipped the sheerest stockings
he had ever seen.

He very nearly lost control. What had happened to the
plain cotton functional garments she'd been wearing the
other day? The ones which he'd sent to the laundry whilst
thinking that she was obviously of the gym-mistress per-
suasion?

He gazed at the slender curves of her body, his hand
unsteady as it followed the path of his eyes. 'You wore
these for me?' he questioned shakily, his fingers splaying
over the barely perceptible curve of her belly.

'Yes.'

'Sweet, sweet torment. You look…wonderful.' He swallowed. 'Quite the most exquisite thing I've ever seen.'

She found herself blushing under that passion-glazed
scrutiny. The underwear had been bought as part of her
trousseau, for the honeymoon she'd been fated never to
have.

Her worried mother had persuaded her to pack them.
'Good underwear always makes a woman feel better about
herself,' she'd urged her. 'And it seems such a pity to waste
such beautiful lingerie.'

Not wanting a row, Sabrina had weakly agreed to take
them and had stuffed them into the bottom of her suitcase,
knowing that she would never have the heart to wear them.
And yet some instinct had urged her to slide them onto her
scented and freshly bathed body before dressing to meet
Guy this evening… Had she secretly been imagining that
shining look of delight as he looked at her?

He dipped his head and dropped a soft kiss on her mouth.
'Get into bed,' he ordered unsteadily, 'while I undress.'

She slid between the linen sheets immediately, thankful that he wasn't expecting her to undress *him*. Why, her hands were shaking even more than his.

She watched as he slowly began to unbutton his silk shirt, and in a reflex action her fingers slid up to clutch at her throat, their tips colliding with the thin gold chain from which hung a ring.

Her engagement ring!

Guy had bent to remove one of his shoes, and Sabrina took the opportunity to pull the sheet right up to her chin and to unclip the chain without him seeing. She was about to place it unobtrusively on the floor beside her when he glanced up to see her shrouded in the sheet, with only her face and bright hair showing, and he gave a lazy smile.

Maybe he was more old-fashioned than he gave himself credit for—because it pleased him to see that she was a little shy. 'You look sweet,' he murmured. 'Very, very sweet.'

'D-do I?' Whereas he looked the antithesis of sweet. He looked strong and dark and very, very aroused. Maybe she should have been frightened by his hard, masculine body, but she was in too deep now. Too enthralled by him—too chained by the honeyed flutterings of desire.

His shirt fluttered to the ground and he left it where it lay with arrogant disregard. But when he turned his attention to the belt that was holding up his trousers, Sabrina surreptitiously allowed the chain to slither like a slim gold snake onto the carpet.

He kicked his trousers off and Sabrina hastily shut her eyes, only to open them to find him looking down at her, a kind of bemused tenderness on his face.

'You *are* shy,' he observed softly.

'A little,' she answered truthfully.

'I like it.'

'Do you?'

'Mmm. But, then, I think I like everything about you. Your golden hair spread all over my pillow. Your skin as white as milk.' Wearing only a pair of dark, silken boxer shorts, he lifted back the sheet and climbed into bed beside her. 'Come here,' he said softly, pulling her into the warm cradle of his arms.

She felt the shock of sensation as they tangled their limbs, his bare, warm flesh pressing against hers, and she gasped with a heightened sense of recognition.

He dipped his mouth to brush against a tiny, puckered nipple. 'I find myself in the curious position of not knowing where to begin,' he murmured. 'Like a starving man being presented with the most fantastic banquet and being completely spoilt for choice.'

'Guy,' she stumbled helplessly, her eyes huge and dark. 'So, do I kiss you?' he mused. 'Yes, I think so.' His lips brushed lightly over hers, there and gone in an instant, leaving her mouth moistly open and expectant. 'Or touch you here?' A feather-light flicker of finger to nipple which made her shiver. 'Yes, you like that, don't you, my sweet torment?'

'Y-yes,' she gasped.

'Or here?' The tantalising graze of that same finger over the moist, warm centre of her panties and Sabrina gasped aloud. 'You like that, too, don't you?'

He looked down, losing himself in the black distraction of her eyes, and felt himself grow so hard that he thought he actually might explode. He struggled to rein in his feelings and then kissed the tip of her nose.

'On second thoughts,' he said thickly, 'we've got all night.'

Guy awoke to the clear tinge of early morning. He narrowed his eyes in the direction of the unshuttered windows to see the first rose-gold shaft of the new sun. The very early morning.

He didn't stir. By his side, Sabrina lay sleeping, her arms spread out in careless abandon across the rumpled bed. He had no wish to wake her—and not just because they'd fallen into a passion-sated slumber only a couple of hours back. No, he needed a little time to come to terms with what had just happened.

Well, he knew exactly what had happened. He felt his mouth dry. They had spent a whole night indulging every single sexual fantasy he'd ever had—and a few more besides. As if there were infinite variations and dimensions to the act of making love that he had never discovered before.

As if the world were about to end and they had greedily needed to discover every sensual pleasure known to man. Or woman.

He swallowed, his heart beginning a rapid drumming at the slow, inevitable stir of arousal. No, if he woke her now it would happen all over again—and, much as he wanted it to happen, he also needed to think.

Because, if he were being brutally honest, he'd behaved in a way that he'd never imagined he could. Had just spent the night making love to a stranger. To a woman who was beautiful, intelligent and engaging—but a stranger nonetheless.

He gazed again at the sky, which was now being pierced by a soft apricot light, and his mouth hardened. He was old enough and experienced enough to know that what had happened between them last night was rare. And yet he'd been reckless, out of control. He'd enjoyed it, yes, but that didn't mean he approved of his actions.

'Mmm!' Beneath the sheet, Sabrina stretched her body sleepily.

Guy felt his heart rate increase as he looked down at the

perfect outline of her slender body and felt the stirrings of desire spring into full and vibrant life. 'And "mmm" to you, too,' he said softly.

Sabrina opened her eyes and felt impaled by that lancing glance of steel-grey as seductive memories of the night danced tantalisingly through her mind. But reality brought with it disbelief. She had given herself to him, no holds barred. So now what? 'What time is it?' she said uncertainly.

'Early.' He leaned over her, his lean, hair-roughened torso just crying out to be touched. 'Is that all you've got to say for yourself?' he teased.

Her doubts fled with the warm reality of his proximity. 'That depends.' Sabrina gave in to temptation and reached one finger up to touch a hard, flat nipple. He groaned, dipping his head to kiss her while one hand trailed down over her flat belly, to where she was hot and moist and ready.

He raised his eyebrows mockingly as he moved to lie over her, dropping tiny kisses on the flutter of her eyelashes and her lips. 'Do you always wake up so pleasingly compliant in the morning?' he murmured, reaching down the side of the bed to open another packet of contraceptives. His fingers came into contact with something hard and metallic and he impatiently shoved it aside until he found what he was looking for.

She could feel the hard tip of him nudging against her and her instant warm, sweet response. Last night he had not only brought her back to life, he'd made her feel his equal. There was nothing she could have done or said that would have shocked him, nor he her.

Sabrina was not about to start making odious comparisons, but she'd never known that lovemaking could be so free or so uninhibited. That it could have so many faces, and so many forms.

With a newly learnt and slumberously provocative pout, she took the condom from him.

'Shall I deal with this for you?' she whispered.

He gave a low laugh of delight, but the laugh was tinged with a certain amount of apprehension. Right then she could do what she liked with him, and he suspected that he would just lie there like a puppy and grin with pleasure. What the hell had happened to his habitual dominance? His need to orchestrate?

'Deal away, princess,' he drawled.

She pushed him to lie back against the pillow, and knelt over him, her long, bare thighs straddling him. 'Quite appropriate, really,' she said breathily, as she slowly inched the sheath down over the hard, silken length of him. 'As you're a dealer.'

'Oh, God,' he moaned. 'God! Why are you taking so long?'

Her fingernails lightly teased at the delicate protection. 'But it's all your fault, Guy—you shouldn't *be* so long,' she teased.

He let her torment him until the condom was firmly in place and then he swiftly lifted her up and laid her on her back. Again he moved above her, but this time there was an inexplicable mixture of emotions on his face, his eyes so dark that Sabrina didn't have a clue what was going on inside that head of his.

'You know,' he mused, and now it was his turn to tease her, the full tip of him nudging against her, 'I always thought that girls who worked in bookshops would be so timid. So demure.'

'And aren't I?'

He smiled, but there was an odd edge to the smile. 'No, you're not,' he groaned. 'You're a very bad girl indeed and you leave me no alternative than to do *this* to you...'

He thrust into her with such power that stars exploded

behind her eyes, and he'd barely moved inside her before she could feel the first slow glimmerings of release. Drowning in honeyed sweetness, she turned her head distractedly from side to side on the pillow as wave upon wave of pure sensation left her shuddering and helpless in their wake.

Guy tried to make it last, but he was lost. This must be some kind of record, he thought as he felt the first sweet tug of his own release.

It was one of the best orgasms of his life, but it left him feeling curiously empty, as though she had taken something from him he had not intended to give. He slowly withdrew from her to find her watching him with dazed disbelief, and his smile was wry as he kissed her.

'Go to sleep now,' he urged. 'Go to sleep.'

And only when her breathing became steady did he slip silently from between the sheets.

# CHAPTER FOUR

WHEN Sabrina opened her eyes again, the space on the bed beside her was empty. She gazed around the room, listening out for the sounds of activity in the bathroom, but there was only silence.

She sat up in bed and yawned, noticing that Guy's clothes were gone. She ran her fingers back through her tousled hair and wondered where he was. Rubbing her eyes, she picked up her watch. Ten past seven. Very early. So where could he be?

She clambered out of bed and went into the bathroom, where she found most things she needed, including a courtesy toothbrush, still wrapped in its Cellophane paper.

She wandered back into the bedroom just as the phone started ringing, and she picked it up with a smile on her face.

'Guy?' she said, thinking how pampered she sounded.

But it wasn't Guy. The voice was female—a husky voice which was edged with suspicion.

'Who is this, please?'

Sabrina wondered fleetingly whether she should give her name. No, better not. 'This is a friend of Guy's,' she answered.

'A friend?' The voice sharpened. 'And where is he, please?'

'He's gone out.'

'Where has he gone?' asked the voice impatiently.

Suddenly Sabrina had had enough. The woman was speaking to her as if she were a chambermaid! 'Who would like to know?' she asked softly.

The voice acquired a sudden brittle ring. 'This is one of Prince Raschid's representatives. The Prince is keen to learn whether Mr Masters has managed to acquire the painting he was so anxious to secure.'

Sabrina very nearly dropped the phone. 'I really have no idea where he's gone,' she said slowly, still reeling from the fact that Guy Masters was doing deals for *princes*. 'I'm sorry.'

'The Prince is paying Mr Masters an extremely large commission—for which we would obviously expect him to be instantly accessible,' said the voice icily. 'And whether or not he chooses to jeopardise that commission by using his time in Venice to concentrate on his love affairs, instead of paying attention to the work in hand, is obviously something which the Prince will be very interested to hear about.'

Sabrina drew in a deep breath, trying to remember that the customer was always right. 'Isn't there someone else who can deal with your query?'

There was silence. 'The Prince will only deal with the owner of the company. Not his minions. Goodbye,' said the woman, and put the phone down.

The owner of the company? The company that paid for this hotel room? Sabrina stared down at the receiver, then walked over to the desk, which was covered with neat sheaves of paper.

She hunted around until she found what she was looking for—a letterheaded sheet of business notepaper stating, 'Guy Masters. Dealer in fine art', and an address in what was probably one of the most famous and exclusive streets in London.

Sabrina felt dizzy. Sick. He had lied. Just a little lie—but a lie all the same. What else had he lied to her about? she wondered as she hunted distractedly around the room for her discarded panties. All those things he'd said. He'd implied…

She drew in a deep, unsteady breath as she clipped up her bra. She remembered his words as she'd gazed up with wide-eyed admiration at the hotel's beautifully faded façade. 'The company pays for it.'

He had deliberately played down his wealth and his influence—which begged the question why? Did he think that if she found out just how rich he really was, he might never get rid of her? And was that why he had disappeared so conclusively this morning, despite knowing that she would probably be feeling vulnerable?

She had just slithered into her panties when the phone rang again, and she snatched it up without thinking.

'Signor Masters, please,' said an Italian-accented voice.

Feeling that she'd already been down this road, Sabrina sighed. 'He isn't here.'

'Could you please give him a message?' asked the voice.

Curiosity overrode caution. 'OK,' said Sabrina tentatively.

'This is Air Executive at Venice Airport. We need him to confirm his seat on this afternoon's flight out to London. A water-taxi has been booked for two-thirty, as requested.'

A flight out *today*?

'I'll tell him,' said Sabrina in a dazed and hurt voice, then replaced the receiver.

The bastard! The cheating, lying bastard! Another lie! How many more would she discover? He had told her that he was staying for a few days—just as she was. Maybe he had always planned to leave just as soon as he had taken her to bed—he probably hadn't reckoned on her falling into it quite so quickly.

She felt the sickening plummet of her stomach as the reality of what she had done began to sink in. She had slept with a stranger. It had been the most heart-stoppingly beautiful night, yes, but Guy hadn't even been able to face her this morning. And that was how much he cared about her. At least he was allowing her to make the decision to leave herself, rather than having to eject her.

Face it, she told herself with a bitter pang of regret, you've been used. The classic one-night stand. But what had she expected? No woman would ever receive courtesy and consideration from a man like Guy Masters—not when she had ended up in bed with him on a first date.

Her heart racing, Sabrina slithered the silvery-blue dress over her head and located first one shoe, and then the other.

She looked around at the sumptuous fittings of the room, feeling more out of place with each second that passed. This was not her kind of world. Guy was not her kind of man. Get out now, she told herself—now while you still have some pride left.

He was probably downstairs on the lookout in the huge marble foyer, waiting until she had gone back to her own hotel and the coast was clear for him to return to his suite.

Pausing only to brush through the tangled strands of her hair, she quietly left the room and located the lift, steadfastly ignoring the rather curious expression of a beautiful young Italian woman until it had reached the ground floor.

Stealthily slinking out, she peeped around one of the giant marble pillars to see, to her absolute horror, that Guy was sprawled out on one of the silk sofas, talking into a mobile phone.

He looked, Sabrina thought, completely businesslike. Miles away. Worlds away. Worlds apart. He'd shaved, put on a suit and smoothed down the hair which she had ruffled with her greedy, frantic fingers during the night. He didn't look remotely like a man who had spent the whole night making mad, passionate love to her. Maybe that had been put in the out tray, she thought, her heart thundering like a cannon in her ears.

She waited until he turned his head, giving her a glimpse of that hard, beautiful profile as he gestured for a coffee.

Moving with a quiet and guilty step, Sabrina quietly left the hotel.

Guy opened the door to his suite, wondering whether Sabrina would still be in bed, telling himself that he would not join her there. After recklessness came reason.

But still a slow rise of colour begin to flush its way along his cheeks, and he moved quietly towards the bed and stared down at it with slowly dawning disbelief. Empty.

He stood very still. 'Sabrina?' he called softly, but even as he said her name he knew that it was futile.

She had gone.

He ripped the covers back, as if they were somehow concealing her, as if her slender frame could be hidden away, but there was nothing other than the lingering musky traces of sex marking the sheets.

His mouth twisted as he dropped the sheet as abruptly as if it were contaminated, his grey eyes growing steely as they travelled around the room.

Her clothes had gone. The discarded panties and stockings had disappeared.

Gone, just as if she had never been there.

A slow pulse began to throb unsteadily at his temple, his gaze not missing a thing as he walked round to the other side of the bed. His eyes scanned this way and that for the note which logic told him she had not left. And at first the glint of gold which gleamed so palely against the silken rug held no interest for him.

Until he realised that she had left *something* behind.

He bent and retrieved the delicate chain and stared down at it with dawning realisation as it glittered in the palm of his hand.

And his mouth twisted into a slow, cruel smile as his fingers closed over it and he dropped it deep into the pocket of his trousers.

# CHAPTER FIVE

THE old-fashioned bell on the bookshop door clanged loudly as Sabrina stepped in out of the rain. The shop was empty save for a mild-looking man with glasses who glanced up, his face brightening into a smile of welcome.

'Sabrina!' he said in delight. 'Welcome back!'

Sabrina tried to match his smile, and wondered if it looked as lopsided as it felt. 'Thanks, Paul,' she said, and slowly began to unbutton her raincoat, brushing off the drops of rain as she did so. 'It's great to be back!'

'So, how was Venice?'

Sabrina quickly turned to hang the dripping garment on the peg, hoping that he wouldn't see the sudden defensive set of her shoulders. Or the swift shiver of memory which had her biting her lip in consternation. How could you ache so badly for a man you barely knew? she wondered. A man who had given you his body, but not his honesty?

But by the time she turned round again she had managed to compose her face into the kind of dreamy post-holiday smile which Paul would be expecting.

'Venice? Oh, it was...' She swallowed as recollections of mocking grey eyes and a hard, lean body swam unwillingly into her mind. 'It was lovely!' she finished lamely.

'Lovely?' echoed Paul, pulling a face. 'This is the place that you wanted to visit more than anywhere else on earth and you describe it as "lovely"? What happened in Venice, Sabrina?' He laughed. 'Did you leave your descriptive powers behind?'

'I'm a bit tired after all the travelling, that's all. I went to see my aunt in Scotland as soon as I got back.' She sat down at the desk and began to flick through the morning's post.

'Yes.' Paul frowned. 'You look a little pale. Like some coffee?'

'I'd love some. I'll make it.'

But Paul Bailey shook his head. 'No, you won't. I'll do it. You look bushed. Sit down and I'll bring you something hot and restorative.'

'Thanks, Paul,' said Sabrina gratefully. She dropped a discarded envelope into the bin and looked around.

It was hard to believe that she was back. That everything was just as she'd left it. And nothing had changed.

She bit her lip again and stared down at the pile of manila envelopes on her lap.

Except her. *She* had changed. In the course of those few days in Venice she had discovered some unbelievable things about herself—things she wasn't sure she liked at all.

And now she was having to come to terms with the knowledge that she was the kind of woman who was able to have a passionate fling with a man who was little more than a stranger to her. A stranger who had left her heart breaking for him.

Paul came back into the room, carrying a tray with two steaming mugs of coffee, one of which he deposited in front of her, together with a chocolate bar.

She shook her head. 'You can have the biscuit. I'm not hungry.'

Paul tutted, sounding torn between concern and impatience. 'I thought that one of the reasons behind you going to Italy was to try and tempt yourself back into eating.' His voice softened, along with his eyes. 'Come on—you can't keep pining for Michael for ever, you know, Sabrina. He wouldn't want that.'

Sabrina quickly put down the coffee, terrified that she

might drop it. For what would the decent and honourable Paul say if he knew how little she had been pining for Michael? She tried to imagine his reaction if she told him the truth about her holiday, and paled at the thought of how his opinion of her would be reversed if only he knew.

'In fact,' said Paul gently, 'I thought you were going to come back from Venice a new woman—wasn't that the plan?'

She lifted her head. 'And I haven't?' she teased him. 'Is that what you mean?'

He shrugged awkwardly. 'Just as slim and even paler—what *did* you do out there?'

'What does everyone do in Venice?' she asked lightly, as she tried not to remember.

Paul grinned. 'You travelled in a gondola, right?'

Sabrina forced a smile in response. 'You bet I did!' And that was how the whole damned thing had started—blinded by a man with night-dark hair and a body which had stirred a deep, primitive response in her. And she couldn't blame Guy for that. She had set the wheels for that in motion herself. Unless she was planning to blame him for his physical beauty and impact. 'Anyway, that's enough about me, Paul. How has business been?'

Paul shrugged. 'So-so. March is slow, as you know, but it'll be Easter soon. Interestingly enough, I had a phone call yesterday from a man trying to track down a rare first edition.'

Sabrina sipped her coffee. 'Oh?'

'That's right. You must have served him. He asked for you. I told him you weren't due in until today.'

'Really?' she questioned absently.

Once she had drunk her coffee, Sabrina forced herself to get back into the slow and rhythmical pattern of her working day and found it comforting. She would put the whole affair down to experience and not let it get out of hand in her imagination. After all, lots of people had holiday romances which ended badly.

If only Guy Masters wasn't such an unforgettable man. If only she hadn't lost her head. But 'if onlys' wouldn't change a thing—they never did.

Fortunately, work soon took over. Maybe that was because she had become an expert in pushing away disturbing thoughts. She settled down to some long-overdue ordering and soon became immersed in that.

She heard the sound of the shop door clanging open and flourished her signature in the order book before looking up and blinking, her polite smile freezing into disbelief on her lips.

It couldn't be him, she thought, even as her heart responded with an instinctive surge of excitement. But the delight ebbed away as quickly as it had come, to be replaced by a sudden wariness when she saw the dark, forbidding expression on his face.

It couldn't be him. But it was.

She was aware of the fact that Paul was working in the storeroom, and composed her face accordingly.

'Hello, Guy,' she said, her voice sounding astonishingly calm considering that the thundering of her heart was threatening to deafen her. 'This is a surprise.'

'Is it?' He leaned over the desk and the male scent of him reached out to her senses, sending them spinning out of control as she registered his closeness. 'So you *do* remember me?' he drawled silkily. 'Wow—*that's* a relief.'

Sabrina blushed at the implication behind his insulting question. 'Of course I remember you! I... We...'

'Had a night of no-holds-barred sex before you did a runner in the morning?' he remarked insolently.

'You were the one who did a runner, and will you *keep your voice down*?' she hissed furiously.

'Or what?'

'Or I'll have you thrown out of the shop!'

Guy's gaze swivelled to where Paul was busy flicking through a card index, and he raised a laconic eyebrow. 'Oh, really?'

She knew just what he was implying. For a man of similar age to Guy, Paul was no weakling, but comparing him to the angry specimen of manhood who stood just inches away from her would be like comparing a child's chug-chug train to a high-speed express. But even so...

Sabrina raised a stubborn chin to him. No matter what had happened between the two of them, he couldn't just march in here like some autocratic dictator and start jeopardising her very livelihood. Not when he'd already taken out her heart and smashed it into smithereens...

'Yes, really!'

He cocked an arrogant eyebrow at her. 'Going to start talking, then, are we, Sabrina?'

'I can't talk to you now,' she stated levelly. 'I'm working.'

'Then when?'

'I don't know,' she prevaricated.

The grey eyes narrowed. 'What time is your lunch-hour?'

'I don't usually take lunch.'

'House rules?' he drawled.

'No, my rules,' she answered stiffly.

'Then change the rules, baby,' he commanded, with a cool arrogance which infuriated her almost as much as it reminded her of his consummate mastery in bed. 'And change them now.'

Sabrina tried to imagine the worst-case scenario. What if she agreed to meet him for lunch—in a city where she had lived all her life and where she was known? She wasn't the same woman here as he had met in Venice. Not by any stretch of the imagination. But what if he managed to reduce her to that same mindless being who just cried out for his touch?

And it wasn't difficult to work out how he might go about that. Surely he would only have to take her in his arms again. Just as he'd done before. She couldn't guarantee that she wouldn't succumb, and how could she possibly come back in here after *that* and spend the afternoon working, as if nothing had happened?

'I eat my lunch here,' she told him resolutely.

He rubbed a thoughtful forefinger over his chin, and the movement was accompanied by the unconscious thrust of his hips. 'Then I guess I'll just wait here until you've finished,' he told her softly, and then deliberately raised his voice. 'Perhaps you could point me to the section on erotic literature?'

'Don't you *dare*—'

'Is something wrong, Sabrina?' Paul came through from the storeroom, pushing his spectacles to the back of his nose, looking with distrust at the tall, dark man who was towering over his assistant's desk.

Sabrina sent a look of appeal up at Guy but was met with nothing but an uncompromising glitter. She knew then that he wouldn't be going anywhere until he got what he'd come for. And that there was no way she could get out of this meeting. She swallowed down her reservations and forced a brittle smile.

'Guy is a friend...' She hesitated on the inappropriate word before continuing, seeing the brief, hard twist of his mouth as he registered it, too. 'A friend of mine. Who has dropped into town unexpectedly—'

Guy fixed Paul with a bland smile. 'And I was hoping to persuade her to come to lunch with me, but—'

'Well, we usually eat a sandwich here—but you go to lunch if you want, Sabrina!' said Paul immediately. 'It'll make a nice change.'

Sabrina shook her head and sent Guy a furious look. How dared he be so manipulative in order to get his own way? 'No, thanks, Paul. I've agreed to meet Guy...after work.' She managed to get the words out—even though they almost choked her in the process.

'Yes, she has. I can *hardly wait*.' Guy gave her another wintry smile, but the hungry look of intent which had darkened his eyes told its own story. 'I'm taking you out for dinner, Sabrina.'

That was what he thought! 'Just a drink will be fine,' she said stiffly. 'My mother will be expecting me home for supper.'

'Your mother?' A frown of disbelief criss-crossed his forehead. Surely she didn't still live with her *mother*?

Sabrina read the disappointment in his eyes, and pride and fury warred inside her like a bubbling cauldron. What had he expected? A reenactment of that night in Venice? A half-finished meal and she would fall back into bed with him?

'Yes,' she said, with a demure flutter of her eyelashes. 'I live with my mother.'

'And what time do you finish?'

'Five-thirty.'

'I'll be here,' he promised, on a note of silky threat. 'Waiting.'

'I'll look forward to it,' she responded furiously.

Guy forced himself to give his cool, polite smile as he left the shop. But inside he was raging. *Raging.*

He should have just forgotten all about her. That was what he had told himself over and over on the plane coming back from Italy. He didn't know what had possessed him to track her down like some kind of amateur sleuth. Because, yes, there were a few questions he would like a few honest answers to—but common sense had told him just to cut his losses and run. She was trouble, and he couldn't for the life of him work out why.

He should have just posted her the chain and the ring with a cynical note attached saying, 'Thanks for the memory.'

And left it at that.

But he had been driven by a compulsion to see her again and to challenge her—a compulsion he was certain was driven by nothing more than the fact that she had given him the best sex of his life.

But maybe that had been *because* she'd been a stranger, not *in spite of* that fact. Because she'd had no expectations of him. Or any knowledge. She'd judged him as a man— a well-paid employee, true, but not as a man with megabucks. She had responded to him in the most fundamental way possible, and he to her. It had left him shaken, seeking some kind of explanation which would enable him to let the memory go.

She had been honest and open and giving in his bed— so why the secrets? The hidden chain and a ring which was almost certainly an engagement ring. Why the sudden and dramatic exit—like something out of a bad movie?

Guy walked around Salisbury dodging the showers—but not dodging them accurately enough. So that by the time he arrived at Wells Bookstore at twenty-five minutes past five his thick, ruffled hair was sprinkled with raindrops which glittered like tears amidst the ebony waves.

Sabrina glanced up from her desk and her heart caught in her throat at the sight of his rain-soaked frame. He would, she thought, be all too easy to fall in love with. Women must fall in love with him all the time. Leave me alone, Guy Masters, she urged him silently. Go away and leave me alone.

Paul, who was standing a little space away, followed the troubled direction of her eyes.

'Your friend is waiting,' he said carefully. 'You'd better go.'

Sabrina turned to him, her eyes beseeching him. 'I know what you're thinking.'

Paul shrugged. 'It's not my place to say anything about your private life, Sabrina—but it *is* very soon after Michael, isn't it? Just take it easy, that's all.'

Guilt smote at her with a giant hand. 'He's just a friend.'

Paul gave her an awkward smile. 'Sure he is,' he said, as though he didn't quite believe her. 'Look, it's none of my business.'

'No.' She picked up her coat from the hook. 'I'll see you in the morning, Paul. Goodnight.'

Through the window Guy watched her shrugging her raincoat on, unable to stop himself from marvelling at the innate grace of her movements. She moved like a dream, he thought—all long, slender limbs and that bright, shiny hair shimmering like sunlight in the grey of the rainy afternoon.

He remembered the way she had straddled him, her pale, naked thighs on either side of his waist, and he felt the first uncomfortable stirrings of desire—until he reminded himself that that was not why he was here.

Sabrina pushed the door open and thought how chilly Guy's grey eyes looked, and how unsmiling his mouth. She told herself that this would be one short evening to get through and then she need never see him again. He had lied to her, she told herself bitterly.

'Where would you like to go?' she questioned.

'You live here.' He shrugged. 'How the hell should I know?'

'I meant do you just want coffee—or a drink?'

He remembered that night in Venice and the lack of interest with which he'd greeted the wine. Yet tonight he could have willingly sunk a bucketful of liquor. 'A drink,' he said abruptly.

Me, too, she thought as she led the way across a cobbled courtyard to one of the city's oldest pubs.

Inside, a log fire blazed at each end of the bar and the warmth hit her like a blanket.

'Go and find a seat,' he instructed tersely. 'What do you want to drink?'

'B-brandy.' She shivered violently, despite the heat of the room.

She found a table far away from the others. She suspected that their conversation wouldn't be for general consumption. Then she slipped her coat off and sat there waiting for him, her knees glued primly together—like a girl who had just been to deportment lessons.

He brought two large brandies over to the table and sat down opposite her, aware of the way that she shrank back when their knees brushed.

'Oh? So shy, Sabrina? Don't like me touching you?' He held his glass up in a mocking toast. 'Isn't that a little like shutting the stable door after the horse has bolted? You weren't so shy in my bed, were you, my beauty?'

She gulped down some brandy, the liquid burning welcome fire down her throat, and her cheeks flushed with indignant heat. 'Did you bring me here just so you could insult me?' she demanded. 'Is that what you'd like, Guy?'

He shook his dark head and sipped his own drink more sparingly, surveying her over the rim of his glass with eyes which gave nothing away. 'Not at all.' But he bit back the unexpectedly explicit comment about what he *would* like.

She put the glass down, feeling slightly dizzy with the impact of the burning liquor on an empty stomach. 'What, then?'

He dipped his hand deep into his trouser pocket, aware that her eyes instinctively followed the movement. Aware, too, that she certainly wasn't immune to him either. He watched with fascination as her eyes darkened and he could sense that she was resisting the desire to run her tongue over her lips.

'Recognise this?' he asked casually, as he withdrew the thin gold chain with the pretty little ring and dropped it on the polished surface of the table in front of her.

Sabrina's heart pounded with guilt and shame. 'Don't insult me even more by asking me questions like that!' she said bitterly. 'Of course I recognise it! It's mine—you know it's mine! I left it in your bedroom!'

It lay like an omen before them.

'Then why hide it from me?'

She opened her mouth to deny it, but could not. He knew. He was an intelligent man. She was cornered, and she reacted in the same way that all trapped creatures reacted. She attacked. 'You lied to me, too!' she accused.

His eyes narrowed. 'When?'

'You implied that you were *employed* by the company—you didn't tell me you owned it!'

He nodded and his eyes took on a hard, bright glitter. 'Yes, I heard about your discussion with Prince Raschid's emissary.'

'She insulted me!'

'So I believe.' His lips flattened into a forbidding line.

'She was jealous,' said Sabrina slowly, as she recognised now the emotion which had made the woman's voice so brittle. 'Jealous that I was in your bedroom.'

'Yes.' His gaze didn't waver.

'Have you slept with her, too?'

'That's none of your business!' he snapped, but something about the dark horror written in her eyes made him relent. 'Of course I haven't slept with her! She's a business acquaintance I've met on barely half a dozen occasions!'

'And you met me once,' said Sabrina hollowly.

'That's different!' But he didn't pause to ask himself why.

'So why did you lie to me about owning the company?'

He paused deliberately and met her eyes with a bitter challenge. 'I wanted to be sure that it was me you were turned on by, and not all the trappings.'

'As though I'm some kind of cheap little gold-digger, you mean?' Sabrina glared at him. 'And you lied to me about when you were leaving Venice, too!' she accused.

He raised a dark, arrogant eyebrow. 'Did I?'

'You know you did! You told me you were staying for a few days, yet the airport said you had a flight booked out that afternoon!'

He gave her a look of barely concealed impatience. 'Oh, *that*!' he said dismissively. 'So what? Flights can usually be changed.'

'And if they can't?' she challenged.

'Then you buy another ticket.' His eyes glittered. 'A small price to pay under the circumstances.'

The cool, arrogant statement told her in no uncertain terms his true opinion of her, and Sabrina stared at him with hurt and anger in her eyes. 'These particular circumstances being sex with a stranger, you mean?'

He smiled. He certainly preferred her fighting and spitting to that lost look of despair she'd worn when they'd first walked in here. 'You were there, too, Sabrina. That's what we did—had sex.'

'Yes,' she said bitterly, thinking that he didn't even respect her enough to dress up what had happened by calling it lovemaking.

'And you still haven't answered my question,' he observed coolly. 'About the ring.'

Shakily, she grabbed her glass from the table and drank from it.

He wondered whether she was aware that her tiny breasts

moved with such sweetness beneath the fine sweater she wore. A pulse began to beat insistently at his temple and he jabbed an angry finger at the chain. 'So why hide it from me, Sabrina?'

She stared down into the trickle of brandy left in her glass and started to feel nervous. 'Can I have another drink, please?'

'No, you bloody well can't!' He didn't take his gaze from her downcast head. 'Sabrina? I'll ask you again. *Why hide it from me?*'

'I d-don't know.'

'Oh, yes, you do.' He sucked in a deep, painful breath. 'Is it an engagement ring?'

Well, now he would know what type of woman she really was. 'Yes. Yes, it is. You know it is!'

He nodded, unprepared for the jerking pain of jealousy. And a bright, burning anger—as fierce as anything he had ever experienced. It pierced like an arrow through his heart. He tried to stay calm, but it took every shred of self-restraint he possessed. 'I see.'

There was something so wounding about the way he said those two empty words that Sabrina looked at him with a question in her eyes.

'Now I understand,' Guy said heavily. He pushed the chain across the table towards her and gave a hollow, humourless laugh. 'You must have had a lot of explaining to do.'

She stared back at him in genuine confusion. 'Explaining?'

He leaned back in his chair a little, as if close proximity to her might taint him. Or tempt him. 'Well, yes. Hell, I know you're a *liberal* woman, Sabrina—you certainly proved that—but surely your fiancé would be a little jealous if he found out about your little *lapse*?' His mouth curved. 'Though maybe not. Maybe you're the kind of couple who play away.' He lowered his voice into a sexy, insulting whisper. 'Then get turned on by telling each other all about it. There are couples like that, or so I believe.'

The blood left Sabrina's face and she stared at him in horror, scarcely able to make any sense of his words. She would have risen to her feet and walked out there and then, except that her legs felt so unsteady she didn't think she would be able to stand properly. 'How d-dare you insult me?' she whispered.

'You're honestly asking how I dare?' His eyebrows disappeared into the still damp strands of his ebony hair. But now it was his turn to look outraged as he leaned forward, his voice little more than a harsh, accusing whisper. 'Quite easily, actually. When you meet a woman and she does what you did to me that night, it's kind of *disappointing* to discover that she's got some poor sucker of a fiancé waiting on the sidelines.'

His mouth twisted as his anger drove him on remorselessly. 'Maybe you were bored with him, huh? Or were on the lookout for someone a little more...*loaded*.'

He deliberately gave the taunt two meanings, and his dark gaze flickered insultingly in the direction of his lap, seeing her flinch as her eyes followed his. And then he shifted in his seat, angry and uncomfortable, realising that he was starting to get turned on. What the hell did she *do* to him? 'Was that it?' he snarled. 'Were you looking for someone with a little more to offer than your home-spun boy?'

Sabrina felt sick and she shook her head, unable to speak. But he didn't seem to be expecting an answer because he ploughed on, a hard, clipped edge of rage to his voice.

'So what did you tell him? Did you describe in full and graphic detail the things I did to you? The things you did to me? Just what *did* you tell him, Sabrina?'

The unwitting inappropriateness of his question brought

her a new kind of strength, and she wanted to reach out
and to wound him, just as he had wounded her.

'Nothing!' she choked out. 'I didn't tell him anything! I
couldn't, could I? Because he's dead, you see, Guy! Dead,
dead, *dead*!'

And the spots which danced before her eyes dissolved
into rainbows, and then, thankfully, into darkness.

# CHAPTER SIX

GUY knew that Sabrina was going to faint even before the great heavy weight of her eyelids flickered to slump over her eyes. The colour blanched right out of her face and she swayed, slender and blonde as a blade of wheat.

He caught her just before she slid to the ground, pushing her head down to her knees while with his other hand he reached round to undo the top button of her shirt. He felt her wriggle beneath his fingers.

She groaned. 'Guy—'

'Don't try to say anything.' His words were controlled and clipped as he rubbed the back of her neck, while inside his mind raced. A dead fiancé. His eyes narrowed. Why the hell hadn't she told him that right at the beginning?

Sabrina felt dizzy, dazedly aware that the other customers must be staring at her and knowing that the last thing she wanted was to attract more attention to herself. She needed to get out of here. And fast. But Guy's fingers were distracting her so. She tried ineffectually to shrug off the fingertips which massaged so soothingly at the nape of her neck.

He felt her flinch beneath his touch and his mouth hardened. 'Don't worry,' he ground out agitatedly. 'I'm not going to hurt you.'

How could he hurt her any more than she had been hurt already? As if his words had not wounded her and left her smarting. She felt the salty trickle of a tear as it meandered its way down her cheek and she sucked in a choked kind of sob. As if she were listening through a cotton-wool cloud which had dulled all her senses, she heard Guy talking to someone else. And then he was easing her head back and dabbing at her damp temples with some deliciously cool cloth.

She opened her eyes with difficulty, startled by the flickering gleam of concern which had briefly softened the hard eyes. 'I'm OK.'

'You are not OK,' he contradicted her, crouching down so that his face was on a level with hers. 'Do you want me to take you home?'

In this state? Why, her mother would start fretting about her—and hadn't she had enough to worry about over the last few months? 'Can we wait here for a little bit?' she asked weakly.

Guy made a slow, glittering appraisal of all the curious faces that were turned in their direction and frowned. 'Or somewhere less public? There are rooms upstairs. Why don't I see if we can use one—at least until you recover.'

Sabrina stared at him in undisguised horror. Surely he didn't imagine for a moment that…that…

'Oh, I see.' Guy gave a low, hollow laugh. 'Is that what you think of me, Sabrina?' he questioned. 'So governed by my libido that I'd take any opportunity to pounce on the nearest woman, even though she's only half-conscious?'

'I didn't say that.'

'No, you didn't have to,' he said grimly. 'The accusation was written all over your face. But don't worry, princess—that's not really my thing.'

Sabrina let her head fall back against the rest. 'I don't want to stay here.'

'You don't have to. Come on, let's go upstairs,' he said, and his arm was strong at the small of her back as he helped her to her feet.

The temptation to just lean back and lose herself in the warm haven of his arms was overwhelming, but Sabrina feebly pushed his guiding hand away from her. Touching him in any way at all was too much like trouble.

'I can do it myself,' she said stubbornly.

He looked as if he didn't believe her, but didn't argue the point, just walked right behind her in case she stumbled and fell.

Gripping the bannister with a grim kind of determination, she was glad when they reached the top and he pushed open the door of one of the rooms.

It was as different from his suite in Venice as it could have been—clean and middle-of-the-road, with a mass of chintz and swagged fabrics—and Sabrina heaved a small sigh of relief. She certainly didn't need reminders in the way of vast, luxuriously appointed beds or priceless paintings.

She flopped down onto the flower-sprigged duvet and heaved a sigh of relief.

Guy stood beside the bed, looking down at her, his face impenetrable as a disturbing thought nagged at his conscience. 'So why the hell did you faint?'

Reproach sparked from her eyes. 'Why do *you* think I fainted, Guy? Don't you imagine that the things you accused me of would make most women feel ill?'

But he shook his head. 'Harsh words are not normally enough to make a healthy young woman pass out.' His eyes threw her a cold, challenging glitter. 'You're not pregnant by any chance, are you?'

She supposed that he had every right to ask her, but that didn't make answering any easier. Especially not when the look of abject horror on his face told her *exactly* what he would think of that particular development.

'No, I'm not.' She lifted her head. 'And please don't imply that that was something in my game plan. We took precautions, remember?'

He wished she hadn't reminded him, though maybe he

only had himself to blame—he had been the one who had brought the subject up. But her defiant words only painted the most gloriously explicit picture of the way she had made the putting on of those damned condoms into some of the single most erotic moments of his life.

He forced himself to express the harsh truth. 'And precautions fail. Everyone knows that.'

Sabrina stared at him as life and energy began to warm their way around her veins once more. And anger. 'Then you should have given more thought to that *before* we made love, shouldn't you?'

'Yes,' he said bitterly. 'Maybe I should—only I wasn't thinking too straight at the time.'

'And just how would you be coping now if I told you that, yes, I *was* pregnant?'

He glittered her a chilly look. 'I'm in the fortunate position of being able to support a child—'

'Financially, you mean?' she challenged. 'Certainly not emotionally, by the sound of it.'

'Anyway, you're not pregnant, are you, Sabrina?' he snapped. 'So it's academic!'

But the nagging and worrying thought was that she *could* have allowed herself to get pregnant, and then never seen him again. Because Guy was right. Precautions *did* fail. Yet falling pregnant had been the very last thing on her mind. 'Maybe we both acted like the world's two biggest fools!'

He didn't agree with her blurted declaration, just continued to subject her to a cool, steady scrutiny. 'So, if pregnancy is not the reason for you fainting, what else could it be? Have you been eating properly?'

'I…yes…no,' she admitted eventually. 'Not really.'

'For how long?' he clipped out.

'It's obvious, isn't it? Since Michael died, I guess.'

Guy felt the flicker of a muscle at his cheek, unprepared

for the sharp kick of unreasonable jealousy. So the fiancé had had a name, had he? 'And how long ago was that?'

There was no way to answer other than truthfully, but mentally Sabrina prepared herself for his disapproval. 'Four months,' she told him baldly.

There was silence. 'Four months?' he said heavily, as though he must have misheard her.

She didn't look away. 'That's right. I expect I've shocked you,' she said. 'Haven't I?'

He gave a bitter laugh. 'One way and another, I've done a pretty good job of shocking myself lately.' Four *months*? His mouth hardened. It threw what had happened into a completely different perspective. He had wondered about her spectacular and uninhibited response in his arms.

So had he just been a substitute for the man who had died? A warm, living body filling her and reminding her of what life should be?

'You didn't waste much time, did you?' he said flatly.

'And here comes the condemnation,' she said in a low voice.

'It was an observation.' He walked over to study an unimaginative little hunting print and resisted the temptation to punch his fist against the flowered wallpaper. When he turned around to face her, Sabrina could see the fire and the fury that sparked from his eyes. 'Why the hell didn't you tell me about it before?'

She bit her lip, willing her eyes not to fill with tears. 'Why do you think?' she said tremulously, before she had had time to think it through.

Guy stilled, his eyes narrowing perceptively. 'Because I wouldn't have made love to you,' he said slowly. 'Because even if it had killed me—' and he suspected that it might have gone some way towards doing that '—there is no way that I would have taken a vulnerable woman to bed and seduced her over and over again! But you wanted me badly, didn't you, Sabrina?' he concluded arrogantly. 'So much that you weren't prepared to risk not getting what you wanted! *That's* why you didn't tell me!'

Sabrina shook her head, and it felt as though it were filled with lead. 'You wanted it, too.' She bit her lip guiltily. 'You make me sound passive—and I wasn't. We both know that. We both wanted it...'

'Badly,' he put in softly, seeing the answering colour which flooded her cheeks. 'Very, very badly. Yes, we did.' He shook his head in a gesture which was the closest he had ever come to confusion. 'The question is *why* we both wanted it—so much that it drove reason and sane behaviour clean away.'

'We were sexually attracted,' she said shakily. But it had been much more than that. She forced herself to forget the warm glow of recognition she had experienced the very first time she had set eyes on him. As if she had known him all her life. Or longer. She stared at his handsome face and tried to sound coolly logical. 'I'm sure that kind of thing happens to you all the time, Guy.'

He shook his head in anger. 'But that's just the point, dammit—it doesn't! Oh...' He shrugged as he saw her disbelieving face. 'Women come on to me all the time, sure...'

Sabrina's smile turned into a grimace, wondering if he had any idea how much he had just insulted her.

'But usually it leaves me cold,' he reflected thoughtfully. 'I haven't had casual sex since I was a teenager.' And never like that, he thought achingly. Never like that.

Sabrina flinched. '*I* don't remember coming on to *you*,' she objected, but more out of a sense of pride than conviction. 'I thought it was *you* coming on to *me!*'

He threw her a look of mocking query. 'It was pretty mutual, Sabrina. You're not going to deny that, are you?'

No, she wasn't going to deny it. She looked down at her

lap, as if the knotted fingers lying there would provide some kind of inspiration.

'I'm still waiting for an answer, princess.'

The resolve which had deepened his voice made Sabrina frown at him in alarm. 'That sounded like a threat!'

He shook his head. 'Of course it isn't a threat,' he said patiently. 'But surely you aren't deluding yourself that we don't need to talk about what happened.'

She bit her trembling lip. 'C-can't we just call it history, and forget it ever happened?' she croaked.

'No,' he said flatly. 'Of course we can't. I think you owe me some sort of explanation, Sabrina.'

'I owe you nothing!'

He wanted to know. He *needed* to. 'Why did you run away the next morning?'

'Why do you think?' She shuddered as she remembered waking up all warm and replete in his bed. 'Because I realised what I had done! And it was never going to be any more than a one-night stand, was it, Guy? Besides, you lied to me—so how could I trust you?'

'And wouldn't it have been more sensible to have thought all this through before it actually happened?' he demanded. 'I didn't drag you back there with me! You weren't drunk!'

His condemnation was like a slap in the face and Sabrina flinched beneath his accusing stare.

'So what was I?' he demanded. 'A substitute? Did you close your eyes and pretend it was Michael?' He ignored her look of pain, remorselessly grinding the words out. 'Any man would have done for you, wouldn't he, Sabrina? I just happened to come along and press the right buttons.'

She met the dark, accusing fire in his eyes. 'You honestly think that?'

'I don't know what to think. It's not a situation I've ever found myself in before. Thank God.' His gaze narrowed into a piercing grey laser, and then he saw her white, bewildered face and felt a sudden slap of conscience. 'You look terrible,' he said bluntly.

'Thanks.' She sat up a bit and sucked in a breath. 'I'm feeling a bit better, actually.'

'Well, you don't look it. 'I'm going to ring down for some soup for you. You can't go home in that state.'

'Guy, no—'

'Guy, *yes*,' he countered, reaching out to pick up the phone, completely overriding her objections.

Soup and sandwiches arrived with the kind of speed which suggested to Sabrina that he might have already ordered them. Had that been the muffled conversation with the landlord she had overheard?

She told herself that she felt too weak to face food, but the stern look on his dark face warned her that if she refused to eat, he didn't look averse to picking up the spoon and actually feeding her!

Guy sat and watched her. The thick broth sent steam over her pale features, but gradually, as the bowl emptied, some of the roses began to creep back into her cheeks. He saw her half-heartedly bite into a sandwich and then look at it with something approaching awakening—as if she had only just learnt how good food could taste when you were hungry.

Sabrina wiped at her lips with a napkin and sighed, aware of the glittering grey eyes which were following her movements with a steely kind of fascination. He hadn't, she realised, eaten a single thing—he'd just sat there and watched her like a hawk.

She flicked him a questioning look. 'You're not hungry?'

'No, I'm not hungry,' he said flatly. 'And I think it's time I got you home.'

She shook her head. He was too potent a presence, who had demonstrated the depth of his contempt for her. She didn't want him invading any more of her space. She didn't need any more aching reminders of just how devastating he really was.

She had blown it with Guy Masters by being too greedy. She should have given him her telephone number and gone back to her own hotel that night.

But nothing could change the fact that she had been desperate for him, driven on by an unrecognisable hunger she'd been unable to control.

Well, it was too late now. What man wouldn't be filled with contempt at what she had allowed to happen, and so soon?

'Why don't you just call me a cab?' she said tiredly. 'I don't need you to come with me.'

'I'm taking you home,' he said firmly. He saw her open her mouth and shook his head with the kind of dominance that brooked no argument. 'Oh, no, Sabrina,' he said softly. 'This has nothing to do with independence, or pride. You're in no state to go home on your own—'

'Yes, I am!' she protested.

'You are not,' he contradicted impatiently. 'And you can sit there arguing with me all night long, but it won't change a thing. I'm not budging on this—I'm taking you home.'

But her ice-blue eyes looked so helpless as she stared up at him that he found himself unable to resist the temptation to brush a stray strand of hair away from her cheek, feeling its warm tremble beneath his fingertip.

His grey gaze burned into her and for one heart-stopping moment she thought that he had relented. She saw the sudden, impulsive softening of his mouth and the way that his eyes had now brightened to glittering jet and thought that he was about to kiss her.

But all he did was open the door. 'Come on,' he said abruptly. 'Time we were out of here.'

He made her sit down while he went to settle up with

the landlord, gently placing her against some cushions as if she really *were* pregnant. And Sabrina bit her lip as an inexplicable yearning to carry his black-haired baby washed over her.

Outside the pub was no ordinary taxi—somehow he had managed to magic up a long, low limousine from somewhere. Sabrina registered the gleaming bodywork with a disbelieving blink as Guy opened the door of the car. She supposed that Salisbury did *have* vehicles like this for hire—it was just that she had never encountered them before. Not in her world.

'Here, put this on,' he said, as he slid into the back seat beside her and buckled up her seat belt, still playing the guardian angel.

'Where are we going?' asked the driver.

'Wilton Street,' she responded quietly.

The driver half turned in his seat and shot a quick look in Guy's direction. 'Wilton Street?' he asked in surprise. 'Are you sure?'

'Of course she's sure!' snapped Guy, and flicked shut the glass partition, immediately distracted by the sweet perfume of her hair.

Sabrina felt the bitter ache of emptiness as the huge car negotiated its way into a tiny road, where the houses were small and boxy, each one looking exactly the same. She stole a glance at the stony perfection of his profile, knowing that she would never see him again after tonight.

And maybe it was best that she didn't. They weren't just from different worlds—more like different universes.

The driver flipped the glass partition open. 'What number Wilton Street?'

'Number th-three,' she stumbled.

Guy heard the tremble in her voice as the car pulled to a halt in front of a tiny house and frowned.

'You're crying!' he exclaimed softly.

'N-no, I'm not.' She gulped, but took the crisp, white handkerchief which he offered her and buried her nose in it.

'Why are you crying? Because I spoke so harshly?'

She heard the self-recrimination which had hardened his voice and shook her head wordlessly as she tried to bring the gulping sobs under control. How could she tell him that she didn't really know why she was crying? That maybe her tears were for Michael—maybe just for herself. Or maybe she was mourning a golden relationship with Guy Masters which had been doomed from the very outset.

He waited until the shuddering of her breathing had slowed down in something approaching calm and then he got out of the car and went round to open the door for her.

'Wait here for me,' he said to the driver.

He led Sabrina up the narrow front path and rang the doorbell. Moments later the door was opened by a woman who was unmistakably Sabrina's mother. She had an amazing pair of identical ice-blue eyes and her hair was still bright—apart from the occasional touch of grey. And Guy had a sudden powerful vision of what Sabrina would look like in her fifties.

Mrs Cooper's eyes flew open in alarm as she saw her daughter's pale and tear-stained face. 'Sabrina, darling!' she exclaimed. 'Whatever is it?' She looked up at the tall, dark man who was supporting her. 'Who are you? What's happened to her?'

'Nothing at all has happened to harm her.' Guy injected calm into his voice as Sabrina shook off his restraining hand and sat down abruptly at the foot of the staircase. 'She's a little upset,' he said. 'Although I suppose that's understandable, under the circumstances.'

Mrs Cooper nodded. 'So she's told you about Michael?'

Again Guy felt the sharp spear of unreasonable jealousy. 'Yes, she has.'

Sabrina wondered why they were talking about her as if she wasn't there. Or why her mother was staring up at Guy with trust rather than suspicion.

'My name is Guy Masters,' he said. 'Sabrina and I met in Venice.' He took a business card from his coat pocket and gave it to her. 'Will you give this to your daughter in the morning?' he said, moving to the staircase and bending his head down so that it was almost touching Sabrina's.

'Ring me if you need to talk,' he said grimly.

And then he was gone and the hall seemed suddenly so empty—so lacking in the strength and vitality generated by that dark, mocking face and that beautiful, strong body.

Mrs Cooper shut the door behind him, and turned to her daughter. 'Are you going to tell me what happened, darling?'

Sabrina shook her head wearily. 'It's too complicated to explain. I'm OK now.'

'Are you sure?'

Sabrina nodded, and slowly rose to her feet. 'Positive.'

Mrs Cooper cocked her head in the direction of the front door. 'He seems very considerate, dear,' she commented curiously, 'your Mr Guy Masters. Are you going to ring him?'

'No.' But Sabrina actually managed a wan smile. *Considerate?* She could think of about a hundred adjectives which would describe Guy Masters.

And considerate wouldn't even make the list.

# CHAPTER SEVEN

*RING me if you need to talk.* Those had been Guy's last words to her a week or so ago.

Sabrina opened her eyes and stared at the blank white space of the ceiling. What woman would want to admit to being needy? And what could she possibly say if she picked the phone up to ring him? *Hello, Guy, it's me, Sabrina. Remember me? I'm the woman you had the one-night stand with in Venice?*

And then what?

No. There was no point in ringing him. No point in anything really, other than trying to get through each day the best way she could.

'Sabrina?'

Sabrina turned over and yawned as she focussed her eyes on the clock on the locker. Nearly ten o'clock. She loved her Sunday morning lie-ins. 'Yes, Mum?'

'You've got—' there was a rather odd note in her mother's voice as she called up the stairs, Sabrina thought '—a *visitor*, dear!'

Some sixth sense warned her. Sabrina sat bolt upright in bed, her baggy Minnie Mouse nightshirt almost swamping her.

'Who is it?' she demanded hoarsely.

'It's Guy,' called her mother.

Her heart did a somersault. 'Guy M-Masters?'

'Why, how many others do you know?' came a shockingly familiar voice.

'I'm still in bed!' she shouted down, feeling the shiver

of nerves beginning to trace chaotic pathways over her skin. There was a split-second pause, and then a sardonic reply.

'Don't worry. I'll wait.'

She told herself that there was no way of getting out of seeing him, even if she'd wanted to. And that was the most disturbing thing of all.

She didn't want to.

Sabrina felt the powerful acceleration of her heart as she quickly showered and dressed.

Instinct told her not to go over the top with her choice of clothes, while pride nagged at her to make *some* sort of effort. If he was simply calling by to check on her welfare—then she refused to have him wondering what he had ever seen in her.

But she was actually shaking as she dressed—in a warm woollen dress which she'd bought at the market, its ice-blue colour matching her eyes exactly. And her knee-high leather boots—absolutely ancient now, but lovingly polished and cared for, so that they had entirely justified their original high price-tag.

Sabrina went downstairs, expecting—no, *hoping*—to feel nothing for him. But she wondered who she had been trying to fool, because the moment she walked into the sitting room and saw him she was incapacitated by his sheer physical beauty.

He looked, she thought with a sharp edge of despair, absolutely wonderful—as wonderful as the first time she had seen him. He was wearing a pair of faded jeans which clung to every millimetre of the longest, most muscular legs she had ever seen. The denim emphasised the jut of his hips and the flat planes of his stomach. And he was wearing a beautiful cashmere sweater in a shade of grey just darker than his eyes. A dark jacket lay heaped over a chair.

There was nothing she could do to stop the primitive

leap of pleasure in her heart. But at least she could keep it from showing. 'Hello, Guy,' she said calmly.

He thought how fine and how translucent her skin was—so fine that you could quite clearly see the shadowed definition of her amazing cheekbones. He had not meant to come here today—he had been waiting for a phone call which had never materialised. He had expected her to ring, the way women always did. And he had been unable to get her out of his mind. Out of a determination to forget her had grown a need to know that she was OK. Well, she certainly *looked* OK. More than OK.

'Hello, Sabrina,' he said slowly. 'How are you feeling?'

'Better,' she told him truthfully. 'Much better.'

They stared at one another, like two people meeting for the first time. Well, maybe not quite like that, thought Sabrina. She knew too much about him to ever be like that. The top button of his shirt was open to reveal the tiniest jagged scar which ran alongside his Adam's apple. A scar she distinctly remembered running the tip of her tongue along, so that his big body had writhed with a kind of reluctant pleasure.

'Would you like coffee, or something?'

He looked at the luscious tremble of her lips and the ice-blue dazzle of her eyes. 'No, I'll tell you what I'd really like,' he said slowly.

It was so like something he had murmured at the most intimate point of their lovemaking that Sabrina felt her cheeks begin to burn.

'I've got the car outside,' he said evenly. I thought maybe you could show me something of the city. I'll park close to the centre, and we can walk.'

Sabrina looked around her, at her sweet mother who could never be accused of being uptight. But the house was small, no, tiny, and it would be impossible to do anything other than stumble out pleasantries that neither of them meant.

'I'll go and get my coat,' she said.

'Wrap up warmly, Sabrina,' said her mother. 'It may be sunny outside, but it's bitterly cold in that wind.'

Guy helped her on with the coat, which had a collar of fake fur. Her hair was loose and spilled into the fur, giving her a faintly glamorous appearance, he thought.

His fingers brushed lightly over her shoulders and he felt the dark lickings of temptation scramble at his senses. He remembered how translucent her skin had been, and that his tongue had followed the fine blue tracery of the veins which laced her tiny breasts.

She looked at him, a question darkening the blue of her eyes. 'Where's the car?'

'It's a little way along the street.' He omitted to say that the street was way too narrow for such a powerful car.

'Not the limousine, I hope?' she asked faintly.

He heard the trace of mockery, and gave a wry smile. So she wasn't particularly impressed by status symbols. 'No, not the limousine.' They began to walk up the road together. 'The landlord of the pub ordered that car, not me. He obviously took one look at me and made an assumption about what my requirements were. I wasn't intending to make quite such a statement,' he added drily.

'Well, you did,' Sabrina remarked as they drew alongside a more sedate, but equally luxurious car. 'My mother said that all week the neighbours have been dying to know who the visitor was.'

He paused in the act of unlocking the door, his grey gaze steady and imperturbable. 'And what did you tell them?'

She managed to return his look, though it wasn't easy— not when it took her mind back to how she had seen it when he'd been in her arms. Stripped of all pretence, darkened and glazed with…lust, she reminded herself painfully. That was all it had been. Lust.

'I said that you were…' She hesitated and now the gaze became laser-sharp, lancing through her. 'A friend.'

His mouth twisted into a cool smile as he held the door open for her. 'A friend?' he mocked.

'What should I have said, then? A lover?'

'That certainly would have been more accurate, wouldn't it?'

'I don't think so, Guy. It's in the past tense now.'

She slid her legs into the car. Actually, she had wanted to say 'acquaintance', because that had seemed more accurate than 'friend', though it hadn't really seemed appropriate either—not in view of what had happened. 'Acquaintance' implied that you didn't know somebody terribly well, and yet she knew Guy Masters exceedingly well. Sabrina swallowed. In certain respects, anyway.

She kept her eyes fixed straight ahead while he drove into the city and parked. And in the dim, ugly light of the concrete car park he looked down at her.

'You haven't asked me why I'm here,' he said suddenly.

'Maybe I'm afraid of what your answer will be.' She lifted her shoulders a little. 'Why *are* you here?'

'That's just it.' He gave a short laugh and shook his head as he locked the car doors. 'I don't know!'

With a chill wind blowing in their faces, they walked right into the centre of the city, with the cathedral spire dominating the skyline and drawing them in like a magnet.

'Want to go inside?' she asked softly.

He glittered her a dark smile. 'You know I do.'

Yes, she had known that, just as she instinctively knew that he didn't want a guided tour, not today. The stiff set of his shoulders said, *Stay away*, quite clearly.

So she walked around the huge empty cathedral with him, quickly turning away when he paused to stare up at the altar and an indescribable sadness seemed to harden his beautiful face into stone.

And that was grief, she recognised painfully, a grief too bitter to intrude into.

Outside, the wind whipped her hair into ribbons which curled over her cheeks and Guy found his fingers itching to brush them away.

'I'll drive you home,' he said abruptly.

She felt the sinking sensation of disappointment. 'OK,' she agreed.

But as he drew up at the end of her street he made no move, taking the key out of the ignition and turning to look at her.

'So what happened?' he asked quietly. 'To Michael?' he persisted softly. 'How did he die?'

There was silence.

'It was a car crash,' she said eventually. 'He wanted to go out for the evening, and I didn't. We were supposed to be saving up. He tried to change my mind, but I wouldn't. He...' This bit was hard, but she forced herself to continue. 'He said that I was a control freak.'

His eyes narrowed with interest. 'A control freak?' he echoed softly. 'Is that so?'

She supposed that he didn't believe her, and how could she blame him? She hadn't exactly behaved like that around him, had she? 'Well, that's the most peculiar thing—I *do* like to be in control, yes. Normally.'

'And so do I,' he said, his voice as bitter as the recrimination in his eyes. 'Perhaps we just bring out the worst in each other.'

And the best, she thought suddenly. The very best.

'We had a row,' she remembered, her voice slowing painfully. 'A blazing row. And Michael got angry and he stormed out, and...and...that's when he crashed. He was killed instantly.'

Guy nodded, his grey eyes narrowing perceptively. 'Oh, I see,' he said slowly. 'So you carry all the guilt, as well as the grief, do you, Sabrina?'

'If only I hadn't been so rigid,' she said bitterly. 'If I'd gone with him then it might not have happened.'

'And it just might. That's a pretty heavy burden to carry, you know, Sabrina. What with that and our little fling you could soon find that feeling guilty becomes too much of a habit.'

She unclipped her seat belt angrily. 'I don't have to stay here and listen to—'

The truth?' he drawled, and something in the way he said it stopped her in her tracks.

'Do you think I feel good about myself?' she demanded. 'Letting a man who was virtually a stranger make love to me, and so soon—'

And so thoroughly, he thought longingly. 'Yeah, yeah, yeah,' he interrupted coolly. 'I thought we'd already done the regret trip, Sabrina.'

'*We?*' she queried. 'You mean you feel bad about what happened, too?'

'What do *you* think?'

Sabrina looked down at her lap. So now she knew.

'I don't know anything about you,' she realised aloud, but he shook his head.

'Oh, yes, you do,' he said softly. 'You haven't seen my flat, or met my family, or seen where I work—but none of that is important. You've seen me at my most—' He bit the word out as if he didn't like it very much. 'Exposed.'

'Like every woman you've been to bed with, you mean?'

He shook his head. 'That night was something outside my experience. Like you, Sabrina, I like to be in control—and on that occasion I most definitely wasn't.'

'Guy,' she said suddenly, and something in the way she said it made his eyes narrow.

'What?'

'Who were you thinking about—back there in the cathedral?'

He stilled. Usually he would have blanked such an intrusive question, but hadn't he just been asking her questions just like that?

'I was thinking about my father,' he said slowly, feeling her suck the admission from him. 'He died a long time ago,' he said, and then his face hardened. 'But we're not here to talk about me, are we?'

'Apparently not.' She shrugged listlessly.

'What you need to face up to now is that it *happened*! Everything. Michael died and we made love all night long, and however much you might want to unwish that—you can't. Fact. End of story. The important question is where do you go from here?'

'I don't know,' she admitted brokenly.

His mouth tightened as he saw the dark shadows thrown onto her pale skin by her sharpened cheekbones. 'I'm taking you out to lunch,' he said grimly.

She shook her head, more tempted than she should have been. 'I can't. I usually have lunch with my mother on Sundays.'

'Then bring her along.'

'Are you sure?'

'Why not? She eats lunch, doesn't she?'

Sabrina nodded, surprised and pleased. Michael wouldn't have dreamed of issuing such an invitation—he'd seen parents as nothing but authority figures, just hell-bent on stopping you enjoying yourself. 'I'm sure she'd be delighted,' she said truthfully.

'Then let's go and find her,' he said, still in that same grim voice.

Sabrina's mother was as pleased by the invitation as her daughter had anticipated, especially when Guy chose a restaurant on the very edge of the city, one which neither of the two women had ever visited before.

'Oh, we couldn't possibly—it's much too expensive!' protested Mrs Cooper.

'No, it's not,' said Guy patiently.

'And we'll never get a table,' put in Sabrina.

The grey eyes glittered. 'Want to bet?'

And of course he got a table—how could she have ever doubted for a moment that he wouldn't? Men like Guy Masters always got tables.

Sabrina tried very hard to eat her shrimp salad and lobster with some element of appetite, but it was unbelievably difficult to concentrate on the food when there was such a distraction on the other side of the table.

Her eyes kept straying to the dark gleam of Guy's hair as he sat and chatted to her mother. The top two buttons of his shirt were undone and she could just see the faint shadowing where the dark hair began.

She wiped a damp palm over the napkin which lay on her lap. What on earth would her mother say if she had any idea that the man who was chatting to her so companionably had ravished her daughter more than she'd believed it possible for a woman to be ravished.

Guy studied her from over his wineglass, suddenly registering her tense silence. 'You're very quiet, Sabrina,' he observed.

'Oh, she's quiet like that a lot of the time,' said Mrs Cooper. 'Can't seem to snap out of it, can you, darling?'

'I don't think Guy particularly wants to hear, Mum,' said Sabrina warningly.

But Mrs Cooper was only just warming to her subject. 'I'm dreadfully sorry that Michael is dead—of course I am—and it's hit her very hard, as you would expect.'

Sabrina didn't dare meet Guy's eyes for fear of the derision she might find there. Grief-stricken people didn't tend to behave in the way she had behaved.

'I know what it's like myself,' said Mrs Cooper, and she reached over and patted Sabrina's head. 'After my husband left me, people always saw me just as a divorcee—not as Maureen Cooper in her own right.'

Guy nodded. So Sabrina had no father either.

'No one will give the poor girl a chance to get over it. And the trouble is that this is where she grew up. Everyone knows her, and everyone knew Michael—and she can't escape from their memories. I think she should get out and have a little fun. That's why I persuaded her to go to Venice—she'd always wanted to go there—but when she came back she looked worse than ever.'

'Have you quite finished, Mum?'

'Can't you get away somewhere?' queried Guy thoughtfully.

'Like where?' She met the stormy challenge of his gaze. She had tried fleeing to Venice and look where *that* had got her.

'How about London? That's where most people want to go.'

'London's expensive,' said Sabrina defensively. 'And I don't earn very much. And, besides, I don't really feel like going into a city where I don't know anyone.'

'But you know me, Sabrina,' came the surprising response.

She violently began spearing at a piece of lobster.

'You know you can always come and stay with me.' He'd spoken the words aloud before he'd realised their implication.

For a second Sabrina froze, and then slowly lifted her head to gaze at him in disbelief. 'What did you say?' she whispered.

'I have a flat,' he said. 'A big flat—plenty big enough

to accommodate another person. Come and use the spare room for a while.'

She thought of sharing a flat with him, even temporarily, and her heart began to bang against her ribcage—until she forced herself to quash the hopeless dream and replace it with reality. 'It's a crazy idea,' she said woodenly. 'I don't have a job to go to.'

'So find one.' He shrugged.

'It isn't as easy as that, Guy,' said Mrs Cooper gently.

Sabrina found herself thinking that Wells did have another branch, in the capital, but loyally she found herself confirming her mother's words. 'No, it isn't.'

Guy stirred his coffee, as if he didn't really care, and Mrs Cooper got up from the table and beamed. 'Will you excuse me for a minute?'

Guy rose to his feet until Mrs Cooper had disappeared, and Sabrina thought what impeccable manners he had. She stared across the table at him as he sat back down. 'It's very…kind of you, Guy, but you know very well I can't accept your offer.'

He coolly returned her stare. 'Do I?'

She narrowed her eyes in frustration. 'Don't be so obtuse.'

'Then don't be so damned evasive—and come right out with what it is you want to say!'

Surely he wasn't really expecting her to say it out loud. But, from his unhelpful silence, he clearly was. Reminding herself that they had already been as intimate as any couple could be, Sabrina drew in a deep breath.

'How could I come and stay with you, not knowing—' she met his gaze without flinching '—whether we…we…'

'Oh, for God's sake!' he snapped, as the meaning of her words became clear to him. 'Do you really think that I'm about to start extracting rent in the form of sexual favours?'

'That wasn't what I said!'

'That's what you meant, though—isn't it?'

She shook her head, but without conviction.

He leaned back in his chair and looked at her speculatively. 'You told me you like to be in control, didn't you? Is that why you're afraid to come? Afraid that you'll lose it again around me? Scared to risk it?'

She met the challenge in his eyes. 'Do you think you're so irresistible?'

'I don't know. Maybe that's something we should both find out. Maybe we both need this opportunity to redeem ourselves.'

She stared at him in confusion. 'Redeem ourselves?'

'Sure. This is the perfect opportunity to demonstrate that we're not completely ruled by our hormones—'

'That's a very nice way to put it!'

'Sabrina, there isn't,' he told her bluntly, 'a *nice* way to put it.'

'So you're saying that the relationship will be platonic?'

'No, that's not what I'm saying at all,' he countered. 'I'm not promising anything.'

Sabrina began to get a glimmering of understanding about what he meant. Put two people who were sexually attracted to each other in a flat, and in the end it all came down to who cracked first. And who didn't. Control, that was what this was all about. Power and control. But she said nothing more as her mother had begun to walk back towards the table.

Nothing more was said on the subject during the drive back to her house, and Sabrina felt an unwilling sense of emptiness as Guy said goodbye to her mother, then turned to her, his enigmatic grey eyes glittering darkly.

'Goodbye, Sabrina.'

'Goodbye, Guy. Thanks for lunch.'

He gave a brief hard smile before climbing into his car.

Sabrina and her mother stood and watched the powerful car move away.

'You aren't going to go, are you, darling?' asked Mrs Cooper. Sabrina carried on looking, even though the tail-lights had long since disappeared.

'I don't know, Mum,' she said honestly. 'I just don't know.'

# CHAPTER EIGHT

SABRINA'S pulse was hammering as she punched out the number, and it hammered even more when the connection was made and a rich, deep voice said, 'Guy Masters.'

She opened her mouth but no words emerged.

The voice sounded impatient now. 'Guy Masters,' he repeated irritatedly.

'Guy. It's me—Sabrina.'

There was a two-second pause which seemed like an eternity.

'Sabrina Cooper,' she rushed on. 'Remember? We met—'

'Yes, of course I remember you, Sabrina. How are you?'

For a moment she was tempted to hang up and forget the whole stupid idea, but she had spent the last few weeks changing her life around. She couldn't back out now.

'I've managed to get a transfer!' she said, and then, in case he had completely forgotten his proposal, rushed on, 'To the London branch of Wells. They've said I can work there for six weeks. The bookshop,' she added, just in case he had forgotten *that*.

'Oh.' There was a pause. 'Good. So, when are you coming to stay?'

He *did* remember. Thank God. 'I can start first thing on Monday.' Sabrina crossed the fingers of her left hand and pulled a ghastly grimace at herself in the mirror. 'If it's all right with you, I thought I'd come on Sunday afternoon.'

'*This* Sunday?'

'If that's a problem—'

'No.' The deep voice sounded thoughtful. 'No, that shouldn't be a problem.'

She thought he might make the effort to sound a little more convincing. Or pleased about it. 'Are you sure?'

'Have you got a pen?' he asked tersely. 'I'll give you directions how to get here.'

She scribbled down his home address, instantly noting that it was in Knightsbridge. So she would be staying in one of London's most affluent areas.

'What time will we see you?'

'We?' she questioned, feeling suddenly frozen by nerves.

'I'm having a few friends for brunch—but they'll probably have gone by teatime.'

'Then I'll come at teatime,' she promised hoarsely.

She struggled onto the train on Sunday with her two suitcases and then onto the tube, where she had to stand for the entire journey because it seemed that the whole world and his brother were heading for Knightsbridge and the museums.

So by the time she reached the outrageously exclusive address which Guy had given her she felt as grimy and bedraggled as a cat which had been left out in the rain all night.

His flat was situated in a quiet square, several streets back from the main thoroughfare of Knightsbridge. In the centre of the square was a gated garden, and Sabrina put her suitcases down and peered in through the railings.

Beneath the trees, daffodils waved their sun-yellow trumpets, and she could hear the sound of birdsong. And despite her misgivings, Sabrina felt a sudden sense of freedom. Picking up her cases with a renewed determination, she walked up the steps of the house, rang the doorbell and waited.

Sabrina glanced down at her watch as she waited. Four-thirty. Most people's idea of teatime, surely? What if the unthinkable had happened and Guy had forgotten that she was coming? What would she do if he wasn't in?

She lifted her finger to the doorbell once more and just at that moment the door opened and there stood Guy. She swallowed down the lump which had risen in her throat.

His dark hair was ruffled, and he wore an old pair of jeans with the top two buttons left undone, revealing a provocative downward arrowing of dark hair. He had clearly just dragged on a black T-shirt which clung to every perfectly defined muscle of his chest. He looked, Sabrina thought with a sudden stab of anxiety, as if he'd just got out of bed.

His eyes narrowed with an unmistakable look of surprise as he stared down at her, and then he said, very steadily, 'Sabrina!'

Her heart thumped faster. 'You *had* forgotten I was coming.'

He didn't miss a beat. 'Of course I hadn't forgotten.' He stole a glance at his watch, which gleamed gold against the faint blur of hair on his wrist, and frowned. Hell, was *that* the time? 'It's later than I thought. Come on in. Let me take your cases. We're just finishing brunch.'

'At this time?'

'Why not?' he said softly. 'It's Sunday. No deadlines.'

'If you're busy I can go away and come back later,' she said, although as soon as the words were out of her mouth she realised how ridiculous they sounded—because where on earth would she go on a late spring afternoon in a city where she knew nobody?

He smiled as he took the suitcases from her, thinking how cold she looked. How she always looked as if she needed protecting. His protection. 'Don't be silly,' he said softly. 'Come on in. You look frozen.'

Well, she was shivering, yes, but that had more to do

with the reality of seeing him in the glorious, living flesh. Of hearing his rich, deep voice. It had only been a few weeks, but it seemed like a whole lifetime since she had last seen him. How could she have so easily forgotten the impact he had on her—as compelling now as when she had first set eyes on him?

She followed him inside, but her nerves were jangled even further when she saw just how amazing his home was—all light and space and breathtakingly big windows.

The walls were painted in some pale, cool colour with modern paintings which might have looked out of place in a period building but looked as though they had been designed to hang just there.

He gestured towards a sweeping staircase. 'I'll show you your room in a minute. Come on up and meet the others first.'

Oh, lord, and here she was looking all grubby and windswept. And whilst Guy looked pretty ruffled himself, he managed to look extremely sexy into the bargain.

There was no time to do anything except hastily smooth down her hair, and she followed him upstairs, trying to look anywhere but at the denim which hugged his narrow hips as he walked.

She could hear the muffled notes of lazy laughter—feminine laughter—and the chinking of glasses, and a sense of apprehension washed over her, even though she forced herself to pin a smile onto her lips. They can't eat me, she told herself. They're Guy's friends.

Guy glanced down at her as he put the cases down. She looked bushed. And fragile. And yet…yet…

A pulse began a slow, heavy dance at his temple as he pushed the door open.

'Come on in and say hi. This is Sabrina,' he announced, as three faces looked up. 'Sabrina Cooper.'

The first thing that registered was that two of the three

occupants of the room were female. And that one of them was a heart-stoppingly beautiful brunette who was stretched out on a huge lemon sofa, painting her toenails and wearing a lazy smile.

She had on a pair of jeans which had been carefully constructed to emphasise every curve of her delectable bottom. As did the teeny-weeny T-shirt which came to just above her smooth brown navel. So, did she, wondered Sabrina with an unsteady thump of her heart, belong to Guy?

'This is Jenna Jones.' Guy smiled.

Jenna gave a polite smile. 'Hi,' she said shortly.

The other sofa was occupied by a man who was looking at Sabrina with interest. At his feet sat the second woman, her hair twisted into a topknot, and they were both drinking champagne out of long, frosted flutes.

'And this is Tom Roberts, my cousin,' said Guy. 'Our mothers are sisters.'

Sabrina looked at Tom, trying to see any family resemblance, but she couldn't. But, then, Tom's face was neither so haughty nor so aloof as Guy's. 'Hello.'

Tom crinkled her a smile. 'Hello, Sabrina.'

'And Trudi Herley—his fiancée.'

'Come and sit down and have some champagne, Sabrina,' said Trudi. 'Have you eaten?' She pointed to the remains of what Sabrina assumed had been brunch, which lay on trays scattered in the centre of the room.

At least they seemed friendlier than Jenna, who hadn't moved and was staring at Sabrina with a decidedly moody look on her face. She looked over at Guy.

'You haven't told us about Sabrina, Guy, darling.'

'Haven't I?' For no good reason, Guy suddenly resented the implication that he *should* have done.

He poured out a flute of champagne and handed it to Sabrina, putting his hand in the small of her back and propelling her towards one of the chairs. 'Go and sit down over there.'

Feeling a little like a marionette, Sabrina obeyed, gulping nervously at the glass of bubbly as he lowered his long-legged frame into a chair opposite her.

Who *were* these people? And who was Jenna, for goodness' sake? That possessive look she was currently slanting at Guy suggested that the two of them were more than just friends. He hadn't brought *that* into the equation when he'd suggested she come and stay with him.

'So where did you two meet?' persisted Jenna.

Ice-grey eyes glittered coolly in Sabrina's direction. 'We met in Venice,' Guy said slowly, seeing her body stiffen in recollection and feeling his own slow, answering response.

Sabrina studied her glass of champagne intently, feeling as naïve as it was possible to feel. Why had she said she would come here? Because there was a part of her which had been secretly hoping that they might fall into each other's arms again? Why hadn't she considered that he had a life she knew nothing about? With other women and other friends? Who obviously were not about to welcome her with open arms. Not if Jenna's reaction was anything to go by.

'Venice?' echoed Tom, and threw him a curious look. 'When you flew over to buy that painting?'

'That's right,' said Guy succinctly, and drained his glass.

'But I thought you never mixed business and pleasure?'

'I don't,' came Guy's smooth retort. 'Not usually.'

Sabrina saw Tom raise his eyebrows in surprise.

'And what were *you* doing in Venice, Sabrina?' asked Jenna.

'I was there on holiday.'

'On your *own*?'

Sabrina saw Guy frown at the question, and something

in the quality of the brief, hard look he sent her gave her the courage to be truthful. Just for once she allowed herself to focus on the pleasure of their lovemaking, instead of the guilt, and a dreamy smile curved her mouth. 'That's right,' she said softly. 'It's the most wonderful place to explore on your own—you never know what you might find there.'

Guy's eyes were arrowed in her direction, their dark glitter telling her that he shared the erotic memory.

'So where *exactly* do you live?' persisted Jenna.

'In Salisbury.'

'Really? Are you on an awayday, or something?'

'Er, not exactly…'

'Sabrina's going to be…' Guy paused, as if seeking an elusive word. 'Staying…with me for a while.'

'*Staying* here?' Jenna's mouth fell open as if he had just confessed to murder. 'You mean she's going to be *living* here?'

'Sure.' He shrugged, and gave a lazy smile. 'Why not?'

Sabrina couldn't miss the swift look of amazement that crossed Trudi's face before she narrowed her eyes, then slowly stood up and nudged Tom with her bare foot. 'Good heavens,' she said faintly. 'Right. Time we were going, I think. Thank goodness Jenna is driving, and not me! Come on, Jen!'

Sabrina drew a deep breath and raised her head, her gaze drawn to the unfathomable grey of Guy's eyes, knowing that she needed to get out of there. Because if Jenna *did* belong to Guy, then she couldn't bear to endure a tender farewell scene between the two of them.

'Could you show me where I'll be sleeping, please, Guy?'

'Would that be the main bedroom, Guy?' Jenna smiled spikily. 'Or the junk room you call the spare?'

There was a brief, frozen silence and then Guy stood up,

his mouth tightening with an unmistakable look of irritation.

'If that was intended to embarrass Sabrina, Jenna, then you've succeeded with honours,' he said shortly. 'This way, Sabrina.'

There was a rather stunned silence as the two of them left the room. He picked up her suitcases, a thoughtful glint in his eyes as he observed her set expression.

Neither of them said a word until he threw open a door right at the end of the corridor to reveal a small room cluttered with a desk, a filing cabinet, an exercise bike and, hardly visible beneath a heap of skiing clothes, a narrow, single bed.

Sabrina turned to face him. 'You weren't expecting me,' she observed, and tried to keep the disappointment from her voice as she took in the general chaos.

He gave a half-apologetic shrug. He was letting her have the room, for heaven's sake—was she expecting red-carpet treatment into the bargain? 'I was snowed under when you rang last week, and I just didn't get around to asking my cleaning lady to sort the place out. Let me go and see the others out, and then I'll come and help you tidy up.'

'I can do it myself!'

'You don't know where to store things,' he said evenly, and walked out of the room before she had a chance to reply.

Unable to do anything until he came back, Sabrina went and stood over by the window, gazing out at the darkening sky, at the city lights which were just beginning to flicker on. She thought of how her life had changed, and was changing still, in ways she had never imagined would happen to a girl like her. And there wasn't, she realised, a single thing she could do to stop it. So, was that fate, or destiny?

She was still standing there when he returned, and as he

walked into the confined space she suddenly became stupidly aware of the fact that he had now done up the top two buttons of his jeans.

And that they were alone.

'What did your friends say?' she asked him.

Guy's mouth twisted. 'Let's just say that they wanted to know more than I was prepared to tell them.'

She dreaded having to ask, but she needed to know. 'And is Jenna your…your…girlfriend?'

He stared at her in disbelief. 'You really think I'd invite another woman to stay with me, without telling her, if she was?'

'I don't know, do I? That's exactly why I'm asking!'

The challenging look was replaced by one of faint irritation. 'I tend to go for a little more communication in my relationships than that,' he said coldly.

'So you don't have one at the moment?'

'One what, princess?' he mocked.

Suddenly she was aware that they were in a bedroom, and that the space between them yawned like a great, gaping chasm. It was the antithesis of the eager way they had fallen into each other's arms back in Venice… No. She wasn't going to put herself through that kind of torture.

'Relationship,' she said doggedly.

God, but she was persistent! 'No, Sabrina,' he said deliberately. 'I do not have a relationship at the moment.'

She realised then that there was something else she needed to know, something which she really ought to have established before she'd come here.

'And won't I…' she lifted her face to his '…cramp your style?'

He looked down at her, momentarily disorientated by that fierce little look of pride. He frowned. 'What are you talking about?'

Her heart was in her mouth as she said it, but she managed to keep her voice steady. 'Well, if you haven't got a relationship, then presumably you're in the market for one—'

'Why, is that an offer?' he questioned silkily, but the surge of blood to his loins made him wish he could take the question back again.

'It most certainly is not!'

'Pity. Actually, I'm *not* "in the market" for a relationship, as you so delightfully put it.'

Was that a note of warning colouring his tone? A polite but efficient way of telling her not to start concocting any little fantasies of her own?

'You might meet someone else,' Sabrina rushed on. 'And prospective girlfriends might be put off by the presence of another woman. Particularly one with whom...whom...'

'With whom I've already had a relationship?' he challenged coolly.

She felt oddly defiant. 'Do you really think that what we had could be called a relationship, Guy?'

'Well, how would *you* like to describe it?' he mused.

As the most wonderful night of her life, that was how *she* would describe it, but tell Guy that and she would see his gorgeous face freeze with fastidious horror. Men judged events differently. A little light passion. No, scrub that. Very heavy passion.

'Things just got out of hand,' she said, trying not to think about the way he'd smiled a secret kind of smile as he'd bent his dark head to kiss her. 'That's all.

As a blow to his sexual pride, it was quite the most exquisite thrust, and Guy very nearly smiled. But not quite. 'They sure did,' he agreed in a sultry murmur, watching with dark interest as the nipples of her tiny breasts sprang into glorious life beneath the sweater she wore. Almost as if they were reaching out to touch him.

He leaned over the bed and scooped up an armful of ski

clothes. 'I'll pack these away,' he groaned. 'And then I'll think about throwing together some supper.'

Guy's idea of 'throwing together some supper' was not what Sabrina understood by the term. For a start, the contents of his fridge could have kept the most dedicated hedonist going for at least a week. Sabrina could see fancy chocolates, champagne and enough different cheeses to stock a delicatessen.

'Do you like smoked salmon?' he asked.

'Er, love it.'

He looked up at her, and frowned. 'Well, do you or don't you?'

'I said yes, didn't I?'

'You sounded unsure.' He gave a little click of irritation. 'Look, Sabrina, let's just get a couple of things straight, shall we? I don't want you agreeing with me for the sake of it—just because it's my flat.'

'OK,' she agreed. 'And while we're on the subject of house rules—'

'Rules?' he interrupted, with a sardonic elevation of his dark brows. 'Goodness me, how very schoolmistressy of you! Are we talking firm and unbending rules, I wonder, or very, very *flexible* ones?'

Sabrina felt a mixture of fury and frustration as she stared into eyes which mocked her. He could stop that right now! 'Oh, do, please, spare me the innuendo!' she snapped.

Guy gave a reluctant smile. Had he actually been worried that all the fire had gone out of her? Not all of it, no. 'OK,' he said slowly.

'I meant rules about things like paying you rent—'

'The rent doesn't matter.'

'It *does* matter,' said Sabrina stubbornly. 'I can't stay here for nothing—and before you tell me that you can afford it—'

'You know very well I can—'

'That's not the point.'

'Then just what is the point?' said Guy steadily, hooking his thumbs into the waistband of his jeans.

The movement distracted her, and suddenly she found his proximity disturbing. More than disturbing. Had she really thought that she would just be able to ignore that blatant sex appeal? 'I'd just like to make a contribution while I'm here.'

Their eyes met.

'Oh?' questioned Guy softly.

She saw the swift darkening of his eyes. 'I'll contribute food,' she told him shakily.

'Food?' Guy queried dazedly.

'Towards the running of the household,' she elaborated.

'Yeah,' he agreed distractedly. 'Whatever you say, Sabrina.'

show you how to...

## CHAPTER NINE

SABRINA was woken by a banging on the door, and her
eyes flickered open for a few dazed moments before reality
clicked in from unconsciousness. Her gaze drifted upwards.
A high ceiling. A beautiful flat. Guy's flat.

'Sab*rina*!'

Guy's voice!

'What is it?' she answered groggily.

'Are you awake?'

'I am now.' She yawned and picked up her wristwatch,
which was lying on the locker. Six-thirty? What time did
he call this? She had never been the best early morning
person in the world. Still in the warm haze of sleep, she
felt too lazy to be inhibited.

'Why have you woken me up?' She yawned again.

'I wondered why you weren't up. Did you set your
alarm? We don't want you to be late on your first day,
now, do we, Sabrina?'

That teasing little lilt set her senses fizzing. 'Of course I
set my alarm! I don't have to be at work until nine!'

'That late?' he drawled. 'I'll have been at my desk for
at least two hours by then.'

'I'll have a medal minted for you, Guy!'

He sounded amused. 'I'm just off now—you'd better
come out while I show you how the security system works.'

Sabrina was out of bed and pulling a face at her tousled
reflection in an instant. She raked a brush through the un-
ruly locks, pulled on her dressing gown and opened the
door.

He was wearing the most beautiful dark pinstriped suit

103

with a matching waistcoat and pure silk tie. The snowy shirt emphasised the blackness of his hair, the faint tan of his skin and the almost indecent length of his legs.

Sabrina couldn't stop her heart from racing at just the sight of him—but it was with pure delight rather than desire, as if seeing Guy in the morning was the most perfect way to start a day. Even though her fingers flew automatically to her chest to clutch together the gaping blue satin of the robe.

Guy didn't miss the movement, nor the tantalising glimpse of pale breast it obscured. He swallowed. 'Let me show you how to set the alarm.'

'Right.' Sabrina tried to listen carefully to what he was saying, but it wasn't easy. It seemed bizarre, crazy, stupid—*tantalising*—for her to be standing half-naked beside him, concentrating fiercely on which numbers his fingers were punching out on the alarm system and not on the delicious lemon and musk scent which drifted from his skin.

'Now, this key,' he told her, deliberately leaning a little bit away from her, because it was more than distracting being this close to the butting little swell of her breasts as they jutted against the slippery satin of her robe, 'is for this lock here. The longer, thicker key...' Oh, God, he thought despairingly, what was she *doing* to him? 'That locks here.' He swallowed. 'Got that?'

'Could you show me again?' She had hardly heard a thing he was saying, and she wished he would just go. But the last thing she needed was for all his expensive paintings and books and furniture to suddenly 'walk'—just because she hadn't had the sense to lock up properly.

'Do you want me to write it down for you, step by step?' he questioned sarcastically.

'That won't be necessary!'

This time she listened as if her life depended on it.

'Understand now?'

'Perfectly, thank you very much.'

He shot a glance at his watch and gave a small click of irritation. 'You've made me late now. I haven't been late in years.'

'Well, you could have shown me all this last night, couldn't you?'

Yeah, he supposed he could have done—it was just that they had opened a bottle of wine during dinner and had then sat and finished it in the sitting room. Bad idea. And Sabrina had kicked her shoes off in front of the fire, perfectly innocuously, but Guy had been riveted by the sight of those spectacularly slender ankles and had found it difficult to tear his eyes away from them. He had never quite understood why the Victorians had considered the ankle such an erogenous zone, but last night the reason had suddenly hit him in a moment of pulse-hammering insight.

He usually did paperwork on Sunday evenings, but last night it had lain neglected. And now he was late.

He glowered. 'I'll be home around seven.'

She looked at him expectantly. 'Will you be eating supper? Or going out?'

He had said that he would meet up for a drink with Philip Caprice—the man who was now working for Prince Raschid—but he couldn't really leave her alone on her first full day in London, could he?

He sighed. 'No, I won't be going out.'

'Then—' she suddenly felt ridiculously and utterly *shy* '—maybe I could cook *you* supper tonight. I'll buy the food and everything—as I said, that can be my contribution towards my upkeep.'

He hid a smile, unwillingly admiring her persistence, as well as her independence. 'OK,' he agreed gravely. He suspected that she would conjure up some bland but rather noble concoction of pulses or brown rice or something. He repressed a shudder. 'I shall look forward to it.'

After her shower, Sabrina went back to her room to get dressed. At least now it looked slightly better than when she had first arrived. Guy had cleared away the clutter on the desk, and had pushed the filing cabinets back against the wall. The exercise bike had been moved from its inconvenient position located slap-bang in the middle of the room. It could do with some decent curtains, she decided suddenly, instead of those rather stark blinds.

She shook her head at herself in the mirror. She was here on a purely temporary basis—she certainly shouldn't start thinking major redecoration schemes!

She dressed in black trousers and a warm black sweater and took the tube to where the London branch of Wells was situated, close to St Paul's Cathedral.

It was an exquisite jewel of a Georgian building, set in the shadow of the mighty church. Sabrina had been there twice while negotiating her transfer and had met the man she would be working for.

Tim Reardon was the archetypal bookshop owner—tall, lean and lanky, with a fall of shiny straight hair which flopped into his eyes most of the time. He was vague, affable, quietly spoken and charmingly polite. He was single, attractive—and the very antithesis of Guy Masters.

And Sabrina could not have gone out with him if he had been the very last man on the planet.

'Come on in, Sabrina.' Tim held his hand out and gave her a friendly smile. 'I'll make us both coffee and then I'll show you the set-up.'

'Thanks.' She smiled and began to unbutton her coat.

'Where are you staying?' he asked, as he hung her coat up for her.

It still made her feel slightly awkward to acknowledge it. 'In Knightsbridge, actually.'

'*Knightsbridge?*' Tom gave her a curious look which clearly wondered how she could afford to live in such an expensive neighbourhood on her modest earnings.

'I'm staying with a...friend,' she elaborated awkwardly.

'Lucky you,' he said lightly, but to her relief, he didn't pursue it.

It was easy to slot in. The shop virtually mirrored its Salisbury counterpart, and after she and Tim had drunk their coffee they set to work, opening the post and filing away all the ordered books which had just come in.

The shop was quiet first thing in the morning, and it wasn't until just after eleven that the first Cathedral tourists began to drift in, looking for their copies of William Shakespeare and Jane Austen.

During her lunch-hour Sabrina managed to locate a supermarket and rushed round buying ingredients. Never had choosing the right thing proved as taxing. She wanted, she realised, to impress Guy.

When he arrived back home that evening, he walked in on an unfamiliar domestic scene, with smells of cooking wafting towards him and loud music blaring from the kitchen.

He moved through the flat in the direction of the noise, pausing first at the dining-room door, where the table had been very carefully laid for dinner for two.

And when he walked into the kitchen, Sabrina didn't notice that he was there, not at first. She was picking up something from the floor, her black trousers stretched tightly over the high curve of her bottom, and Guy felt his throat thicken.

'Hello, Sabrina.'

Half a lemon slid uselessly from her fingers back to the floor as she heard the soft, rich timbre of his voice. She turned round slowly, trying to compose herself, to see him still wearing the beautiful dark suit, the slight shadowing around his chin the only outward sign that twelve hours had elapsed since she had last seen him. Oh, sweet Lord, she thought despairingly. He is *gorgeous*.

'Hi!' she said brightly. 'Good day at—'

'The office?' he put in curtly. 'Yes, fine, thanks.'

'Shall I fix you a drink? Or would you prefer to get changed first?'

His mouth tightened. 'Any minute now and you're going to offer to bring me my pipe and slippers.'

Sabrina stiffened as she heard his sarcastic tone. 'I was only trying to be friendly—'

'As opposed to coming over as a parody of a wife, you mean?'

'That was certainly not my intention,' she told him primly.

The glittering grey gaze moved around the room to see that his rather cold and clinical kitchen had suddenly come to life. 'This looks quite some feast,' he observed softly.

'Not really.' But she blushed with pleasure. 'And if you're planning to get out of your best suit, could you, please, do it now, Guy? Because dinner will be ready in precisely five minutes.'

Neglected work. Late. And now she was telling him to get changed!

Guy opened his mouth to object and then shut it again. What was the point? And she was right—he didn't want to eat in his 'best' suit, which was actually one of twenty-eight he had hanging neatly in his wardrobe. He sighed. 'Five minutes,' he echoed.

He took slightly longer than five minutes, simply because, to his intense exasperation, he realised that she had managed to turn him on. Had that been her bossiness or her presumption? he wondered achingly as he threw cold water onto his face like a man who had been burning up in the sun all day. Or maybe it had something to do with the fact that he hadn't been with a woman since that amazing night with Sabrina in Venice. Hadn't wanted to. Still didn't want anyone. Except her.

Now, that, he thought, was worrying.

The meal began badly, with Guy frowning at the heap of prawns with mayonnaise which Sabrina had heaped on a plate.

'You don't like prawns?' she asked him nervously.

'Yeah, I love them, but you really shouldn't have gone to all this trouble.'

'Oh, it was no trouble,' she lied, thinking about the beef Wellington which was currently puffing up nicely in the oven. 'Do you want to open the wine? I bought a bottle.'

He shook his head, remembering last night, the way it had loosened him up so that he had spent a heated night tossing and turning and wondering what she would do if he walked just along the corridor and silently slipped into bed beside her. 'Not for me thanks,' he answered repressively. 'You can have some, of course.'

'I'm fine, thanks.' As if she would sit there drinking her way through a bottle of wine while he looked down that haughty and patrician nose of his.

Guy saw the beef Wellington being carried in on an ornate silver platter he'd forgotten he had and which she must have fished out from somewhere.

'Sabrina,' he groaned.

Her fingers tightened on the knife. 'Don't tell me you don't like beef Wellington,' she said, the slight note of desperation making her voice sound edgy.

'Who in their right mind wouldn't?' He sighed. 'It's just that you must have spent a fortune on this meal—'

'It was supposed to be a way of saying thank you—'

'And I've told you before not to thank me!' he said savagely, feeling the sweet, inconvenient rush of desire as her lips trembled in rebuke at him. 'Look, Sabrina, I don't expect you earn very much, working in a bookshop—'

'Certainly nowhere in your league, Guy,' she retorted.

'And I don't want you spending it all on fancy food!'

'I'm not here to accept charity—especially not yours!'

'Sabrina—'

'No, Guy,' she said stubbornly. 'I want to pay my way as much as possible.'

He took the slice she offered him and he stared down at it with grudging reluctance. Pink and perfect. So she could cook, too. He scowled. 'Do that,' he clipped out. 'But this is the last time you buy me steak! Understood?'

That was enough to guarantee the complete loss of her appetite, and it was only pride which made Sabrina eat every single thing on her plate. But by the time they were drinking their coffee his forbidding expression seemed to have thawed a little.

'That was delicious,' he said.

'The pleasure was all mine.'

He heard the sarcasm in her voice, saw the little pout of accusation which hovered on her lips. Maybe he *had* been a little hard on her. 'I'm not used to sharing,' he shrugged.

'It shows.' She risked a question, even if the dark face didn't look particularly forthcoming. 'Have you got any brothers and sisters?'

'One brother; he's younger.'

'And where is he now?'

He sighed as he saw her patient look of interest. These heart-to-heart chats had never really been part of his scene. 'He lives in Paris—he works for a newspaper.'

'That sounds interesting.'

He blanked the conversation with a bland smile. 'Does it?'

But Sabrina wasn't giving up that easily. What were they *supposed* to talk about, night after night—the *weather*?

'So, no live-in girlfriends?' she asked.

The eyes glittered. 'Nope.'

'Oh.' She digested this.

'You sound surprised,' he observed.

'I am, a little.'

'You see me as so devastatingly eligible, do you, Sabrina?'

Her smile stayed as enigmatic as his. 'That's a fairly egotistical conclusion to jump to, Guy—that wasn't what I said at all. I just thought that a man in your position would yearn for all the comforts of having a resident girlfriend.'

'You mean regular meals.' His eyes fell to his empty plate. 'And regular sex?'

Sabrina went scarlet. 'Something like that.'

'The comfort and ease of the shared bed?' he mused. 'It's tempting, I give you that. But sex is the easy bit—it's communication that causes all the problems. Or rather the lack of it.' His voice grew hard, almost bitter.

Sabrina looked at him and wondered what he wasn't telling her. 'You mean you've never found anyone you could communicate with?'

'Something like that.' No one he'd ever really *wanted* to communicate with. 'Or at least, not unless we both happened to be horizontal at the time.' He looked at her thoughtfully as she blushed. 'But I have a very low boredom threshold, princess,' he added softly.

He was telling her not to come too close—it was as plain as the day itself. And it was the most arrogant warning she had ever heard. 'More coffee?' she asked him coolly.

# CHAPTER TEN

'SO HOW has your first week been?'

Guy looked across the sitting room to where Sabrina was curled up like a kitten with a book on her lap—she was always *reading*, though he noticed that not many pages had been turned in the past hour. Snap, he thought with a grim kind of satisfaction. He hadn't made many inroads into his *own* reading.

Sabrina met the piercing grey gaze and repressed a guilty kind of longing. How could she possibly concentrate on her book when she had such a distraction sitting just across the room from her?

'I've enjoyed it,' she told him truthfully. Well, most of it, anyway. It wasn't easy being around him, being plagued by memories of a time it was clear that both of them wished forgotten—but at least she had done her utmost not to show it. She forced a smile. 'How do you rate me as a flatmate?'

Guy thought about it. She was certainly less intrusive than he would have imagined. She kept out of his way in the mornings. She didn't drift around the place in bits of provocative clothing—and she didn't leave panties and tights draped over the radiator, which he understood was one of the major irritations when sharing with a woman.

'Seven out of ten,' he drawled, his smile not quite easy. 'And how's the bookshop surviving with its newest member of staff?'

Sabrina wished he wouldn't stretch his legs out like that. 'The shop is f-fine,' she stumbled. 'In fact, it's very similar to the Salisbury branch—'

'So living in the big city doesn't scare you, Miss

Cooper?' he mocked softly, cutting right through her stumbled reply.

'I don't scare easy,' she said, raising a glittering blue gaze, and thinking that it was all too easy to be scared. Scared of her susceptibility to Guy Masters—especially when he looked at her like *that*. Scared of what might happen if he should happen to lazily make a pass at her—because surely *most* men who had already slept with a woman *would* make a pass. Even if they'd said that they wouldn't.

But Guy, of course, hadn't.

In fact, he'd spent the last five evenings behaving as though he had a piece of radioactive equipment in the room with him—keeping a wary and observant distance and occasionally glancing her a look from beneath those sensationally long black lashes. But tonight he seemed edgy.

'Do you want to go out for a drink before supper?' he asked suddenly.

Sabrina snapped her book shut with nervous fingers. 'What, now, tonight?'

He shrugged. 'It's Friday night—it's what people do.'

Anything would be better than having to spend another whole evening watching while she managed to turn reading a book into a very erotic art form indeed. It was all getting a little too cosy for comfort. And Guy had found that leafing through art-world journals had lost most of its allure when he had the infinitely more distracting vision of Sabrina flicking that bright red-gold hair back over her slim shoulders.

But it was a challenge he had set himself and Guy thrived on challenges. He was determined to resist her—and resist her he damned well would. Unwittingly he had taken advantage of her once before, but once had been enough. 'How about it?' he asked.

She thought about the fine wines he had crowding the

vast rack in the dining room. Maybe he wanted to go out because he was bored, just sitting here alone with her night after night. And it was just politeness which had made him invite her to go with him.

'You go out if you like,' she offered. 'I'll stay in. You don't have to have me tagging along with you.'

'You can't sit in here all on your own,' he objected.

She forced a smile. It would do her good. After five evenings she was beginning to enjoy his company a little *too* much. 'Go on! You go, Guy—I'll be fine here. I'll probably have an early night.'

Guy felt an infuriating urge to stay home, yet he hadn't been out a single night this week—and this from the man who was the original party animal. 'Sure?' he asked reluctantly.

'Who else is going?'

'Tom is, and a couple of guys who work with him. Oh, and I expect that Trudi and Jenna might turn up.'

Jenna. Sabrina's smile didn't slip. 'I think I'll pass, if you don't mind. Honestly, Guy, I'm tired.'

Guy rose to his feet, strangely reluctant to move. 'Maybe we should go out for dinner some time?'

She felt a little stab of pleasure, until she reminded herself that it wasn't a date. He was simply making sure that she wasn't bored.

'Dinner?' she asked casually.

'Yeah. There are a couple of clients I need to take out— you might as well come with me.'

'Oh. Right,' she said, her heart sinking despite her intention not to let it. No, it definitely *wasn't* a date—he couldn't have phrased it more unflatteringly if he'd tried. The token female at a client dinner!

He paused by the door and shot her a quick glance. 'Any plans for tomorrow?'

'Not really. I'm working. I work every third Saturday.'

He nodded. 'Me, too. Well, actually, I work *most* Saturdays.'

Sabrina stared at him. 'Why?'

He frowned. 'Why what?'

'Why do you work on Saturdays?' She gave him a slightly waspish smile. He left at the crack of dawn each morning and didn't put in an appearance until at least eight o'clock. Even after five days she had decided that he drove himself too hard. 'You do happen to *own* the company, don't you, Guy?'

'Yes, I do, and I like to make sure that I stay one step ahead of my competitors,' he retorted softly. 'And the only way to do that is to work hard. Number-one lesson in life. Build yourself so high that no one can knock you down. Ever.'

She lifted her eyebrows. He sounded almost *ruthless*. 'Try to be invincible, you mean?'

There was an unmistakable flicker of tension around his mouth. 'It's an achievable goal,' he answered, in a voice which was suddenly harsh.

She was tempted to tell him that he was already top of the heap. And that it didn't look as if anyone was going to knock him anywhere, least of all down, but there was a distinctly warning glitter hardening his slate-grey eyes.

She thought of him as polished and sophisticated, a man who had everything, with his dark good looks and his enormous flat and wealthy lifestyle—and that wasn't even taking into account his consummate skill as a lover. Yet something just now had frozen his face into granite. Had made him look almost savage. Was Guy Masters a man of never-ending ambition—and, if so, then why, when he seemed to have more than most men could only dream of?

'What's so good about being invincible?' she queried softly.

Guy's face tightened. Because it was the opposite of how

his father had operated, with his easy come, easy go attitude
to life and all the devastation that attitude had brought in
its wake. But he had never shared that devastation with any
woman and he wasn't about to start now. Even with Sabrina
Cooper and her warm, trusting smile and tantalising blue
eyes which the devil himself must have given her.

'It all comes down to personal choice,' he said coldly.
'And that's mine.'

Sabrina could recognise a brush-off when she heard
one—and more than a reluctance to open up. From the
daunting expression in those dark, stormy eyes, it was more
like a *refusal* to talk.

Tactically, she retreated.

'Have a nice time,' she said placidly. 'I think I'll have
a bath and that early night.'

Guy had to stifle a groan as some of the tension he'd
been feeling was replaced by a new and different kind of
tension. Images of her long, pale limbs submerged beneath
the foaming bubbles of his bathtub crept tantalisingly into
his mind as his photographic memory recalled them with
breathtaking accuracy. Did she really need to share something like *that* with him?

'Yeah,' he clipped out. 'Do that.'

'Shall I leave you some supper?' she asked. 'I thought
I'd make some risotto—I got some amazing oyster mushrooms cheap at the market.'

Guy scowled. Just five days and she seemed to have
taken over most of the cooking and most of the shopping—
and she insisted on shopping around to save him money—
*even when he'd told her that she didn't need to*. With her,
it seemed pride as much as parsimony—and she could be
so damned *stubborn*.

'You don't have to cook for me every night,' he said
shortly. 'I told you that.'

'But it's no trouble if I'm cooking for myself—'

'I'm perfectly capable of fixing myself some eggs when I get home!' Guy snapped, and turned and walked out of the room, because that hurt little tremble of her mouth was enough to crumble a heart of stone.

Sabrina could hear him slamming around in his room; then the telephone began to ring. She waited to see whether Guy would answer it, but it carried on ringing and so she picked it up.

'Hello?'

There was a pause, and then a rather flustered-sounding woman's voice said, 'I'm sorry—I think I must have got the wrong number.'

'Who did you want to speak to?' enquired Sabrina patiently.

'Guy Masters. My son.'

'Your *son*? Oh, I'm sorry, Mrs Masters, I didn't realise— I'll just get him for you.'

'No, no, wait a minute—just who might *you* be?'

Sabrina cleared her throat. 'I'm Sabrina,' she said. 'Sabrina Cooper.' And then, because the voice seemed to be waiting for some kind of clarification, she added, 'I'm staying here. With Guy.'

'*Are* you now?' enquired the voice interestedly.

'Er, just a minute, I'll get him for you,' said Sabrina hastily, but when she looked up it was to find Guy standing in the doorway, his face a dark and daunting study.

Wordlessly, he came and took the phone from her, and Sabrina quickly left the room, but not before she heard his first responses.

'Hi, Ma. Mmm. Mmm. No, no. No—nothing like that.'

A few minutes later, he came and found her in the kitchen, chopping up her mushrooms.

'Don't do that again!' he warned.

She put the knife down. 'Do what?'

'Answer my phone—especially when I'm *around*.'

'I'm sorry,' she said stiffly. 'I didn't realise I was breaking some unwritten rule, but of course it *is* your flat.' His flat, his territory, his control.

But he didn't appear to be listening. 'And now my mother's asking me eight hundred questions about you. Move a woman in and suddenly everyone's thinking rice and confetti!'

'Well, I can assure you that I'm not,' she told him acidly.

'Me, neither!' he snapped.

She turned her back on him and heard him go out, slamming the door behind him, and she viciously decapitated a mushroom. He was bad-tempered and unreasonable, she told herself. And she must have been crazy to agree to come here.

Guy walked into the Kensington wine-bar where his friends had been congregating on Friday evenings for as long as he could remember, surveying the dimly lit and crowded room with an unenthusiastic eye. He asked himself why he had bothered to come out to fight his way to the bar for a glass of champagne when he could have drunk something colder and vastly superior at home. And maybe given Sabrina a glass, too.

He shook his head. What the hell was he thinking of? He *always* went out on a Friday night!

'Guy!' called Tom Roberts, from the other side of the room, and Guy forced himself to smile in response as he wove his way through the crowded room.

'It's obviously been a bad day!' joked his cousin, as Guy joined him.

'On the contrary.' Guy took the proffered glass of champagne and gave it a thoughtful sip. 'I think I may have negotiated a deal on that old schoolhouse over by the river. It's going to make someone a wonderful home.'

'So why the long face?' teased Tom.

'I guess I'm just tired,' said Guy, and that much was true. Sleep didn't come easily when all you could think about was moon-pale flesh and banner-bright hair and a naked body in the room just along the corridor.

Tom topped up his glass. 'So how's the new flatmate working out?' he asked casually.

Guy could recognise a leading question when he heard one. 'Sabrina?' he stalled, equally casually.

Tom smiled. 'Unless you've moved another one in.'

'I must have needed my head examined!' groaned Guy.

'That bad, is it?' Tom threw him a sympathetic glance. 'She seemed sweet.'

'Yeah, she is.' Too damned sweet. Sweet as honey. That night in his bed—all clinging and sticky like honey. A honey *trap*, he thought with a sudden heat, and drained his glass in one. 'Where's Trudi tonight?' he asked.

'She's on a sales conference in Brussels,' explained Tom. 'She's not coming back until tomorrow.'

Guy nodded. Good. Good. 'Fancy going out for a meal in a while?' he asked.

'Oh!' Tom started grinning. 'Diversionary tactics to keep you out of the flat, you mean?'

'I don't know what you're talking about.' Guy shrugged.

'Oh, we've all been there, mate,' said Tom obscurely. 'There's bound to be a woman sooner or later who gets underneath your skin. It's about time it happened to you!'

'Sorry.' Guy's voice was cool but firm. 'You've lost me.'

Tom put his glass down and narrowed his eyes. 'And you still haven't told me anything about Sabrina Cooper...'

'What do you want to know?'

'The obvious. Like, is she a friend, or is she a lover?'

Guy opened his mouth and then shut it again. What was the point in trying to explain the whole bizarre situation, even to a man who had known him nearly all his life?

Sabrina's reputation wouldn't emerge from it unscathed. And neither, he realised grimly, would his own.

'We're men, Tom,' he said flippantly, 'so we never talk about things like that, right?'

In Guy's high-tech kitchen, Sabrina unenthusiastically cooked her risotto, and then picked at it without interest. She had made plenty. Enough for two...just in case. But Guy still wasn't back. Should she pop the rest into the fridge and cover it with clingfilm? Or would Guy go mad if she did that? Probably. He'd blanched with horror when she'd suggested frying up some leftover potato for breakfast.

After supper she forced herself to relax in a long, deep bath, and when she came out she looked at the clock to see that it was getting on for ten. So, his 'quick' drink was taking longer than he'd anticipated.

She put her bedroom light out and tried to sleep, but sleep infuriatingly refused to protect her with its mantle of oblivion. In the end she gave up trying and snapped on the light and tried reading her book.

'Tried' being the operative word. The words danced like tiny black beetles in front of her and all she could think about was that it was now nearly midnight and all the bars would be closed.

And Guy still wasn't back.

She pulled on her dressing gown and went to pace up and down the sitting room.

By twelve she was getting frantic, and by one she was just about to pick up the phone and call the hospital when she heard the sound of a key being turned in the lock. She flew out into the hall to find Guy with his back to her, shutting the door with exaggerated care and hanging up his overcoat with the other hand.

Sabrina didn't even stop to think about it. She just blazed

right in there. 'Where the hell have you *been*?' she demanded.

He turned round, the grey eyes narrowing to cold chips of slate as he saw Sabrina in her satin dressing gown, her tiny breasts heaving, a look of complete fury on her face. 'I *beg* your pardon?'

That frosty little question should have been enough to stop her in her tracks, and normally it would have done, but, then, this didn't feel normal. None of it did. Surely 'normal' would have meant a complete numbing of her senses until she was properly over Michael?

'You told me you were going out for a quick drink!' she stormed, her breathing coming through in great ragged bursts.

Guy felt torn between incredulity and irritation. 'And?'

'And it *wasn't*, was it? Not quick at all. It's way past midnight—what *time* do you call this?'

'It's none of your damned business what time it is!' he roared. 'I'll live my own life, the way I always have done! I'll go out *when* I want and *where* I want and with *whom* I want—and I'll do it *without* your permission, thank you, princess!'

Through her shuddering breaths Sabrina stared at him, realising just how preposterous she must have sounded. And realising that if she didn't get away from him pretty quickly, she risked making even more of a fool of herself.

'I'm sorry,' she said tightly. 'I spoke out of turn.' She half ran along the corridor and into her room and then pressed her forehead to the door, her eyes closed, her breath still shuddering.

He'd seen the awful whitening of her face and the brief glimpse of terror which had iced the blue of her eyes, and in an instant he'd begun to comprehend just what had motivated her reaction.

'Damn!' he swore softly. Swiftly following in her foot-steps, he went and banged his fist on the door. 'Oh, damn!'

Behind the door, Sabrina froze. Just keep quiet, some instinct of preservation told her. Keep very quiet and just don't answer and he might go away.

'Sabrina! Open the damned door. We both know you can't possibly be asleep.'

She shook her head. 'Go away.'

'I'm not moving from this spot until you open the door and come out and talk to me. That way neither of us will get to sleep and that means we'll both be bad-tempered at work tomorrow.'

You and your precious *work*, thought Sabrina, trying to concentrate on something—*anything*—other than how she wanted to open the door and fall into his arms, and...and...

'Alternatively, I could kick it down,' he promised in a voice of silky intent.

It was such an outrageous proposal that Sabrina very nearly smiled. 'You wouldn't do that,' she sniffed.

'Not unless you make me,' he agreed mockingly. 'So, are you going to open the door now? Or not?'

Slowly, she complied, her fingers clutching onto the handle as if they were petrified, gearing herself up to withstand Guy's fury at her presumptuous behaviour. But when she dared to look up into his face it was to see a look of bitter regret written there, and Sabrina felt the trembling approach of tears. If she weren't careful, she was in terrible danger of exposing all her desperate insecurities to him.

'I'm s-sorry,' she said shakily. 'I had no right—'

'No.' He shook his head. 'I'm sorry. It was the most stupid and insensitive thing to do and, oh, God, Sabrina...' His voice deepened to a caress as he saw her face crumple. 'Princess, don't cry. Please, don't cry.'

'I'm n-not c-crying,' she sobbed quietly, trying simultaneously to push him out of the room and close the door after him, and failing miserably to do either.

Saying something that she couldn't quite make out, Guy just grabbed her by the hand and steered her into the sitting room.

'What do you think you're doing?' she spluttered.

'What does it look like? I'm taking you somewhere where we can talk.' Somewhere that didn't involve a bed. 'I'm damned if I'm going to have you fainting on me for a second time!'

'I'm not going to faint. I want to go to bed,' she said plaintively.

'Well, we need to talk,' he said grimly. 'Or, rather, *you* need to talk, princess.'

He pushed her down very gently on the sofa and covered her with a cashmere throw, which was as light as a feather and as warm as toast.

'That's nice,' she said automatically.

It was also vital, in his opinion, that she cover up. If he wanted to talk to her—or, rather, have her talk to *him*—then he needed to concentrate. And it would be damned nigh impossible trying to concentrate on anything—other than an urgent need to possess her—when that silky robe was clinging like honey to the sweet swell of her limbs and moulding the perfect outline of her tiny breasts.

He sat down next to her and stared into the pale heart of her face. 'It was thoughtless of me. I should have telephoned—told you I was going to be late.'

'It doesn't matter.' She shook her head. 'I had no right to expect—'

'You had every right to expect consideration,' he refuted heatedly. 'And at least a *modicum* of understanding.' There was a grim kind of pause and his grey eyes glittered with self-recrimination. 'And I showed you neither.' He had deliberately stayed out tonight—and he still wasn't sure why—without thinking through the consequences of his actions. 'Neither,' he finished bitterly.

'It doesn't matter,' she repeated, and even managed to raise her shoulders in a shrug, as if it really *didn't* matter, but he shook his head like a man who was onto something and wouldn't give up.

'Why don't you tell me,' he said slowly, 'about the night Michael died? Is that what happened? Were you waiting for him and he never came?'

Something in the burning intensity of his eyes pierced right through the barriers she'd built around herself. She'd pushed the memories of that night to the far recesses of her mind. Deliberately. It had been a defence mechanism to shield her from the bitter pain, and the guilt. She'd refused counsellors and her mother's faltering requests that she open up and talk to someone.

But something in Guy's face completely disarmed her, and her words of defiance and denial died on her lips.

'OK, I'll tell.' She nodded her head slowly. 'I'll tell you everything.' There was a pause while she struggled to find the right words. 'Like I said, Michael wanted to go out that night and I didn't, and it was more than about the fact we couldn't afford it. It was a filthy night. The weather was awful...snow and ice.'

She took a slow, shuddering breath and stared at him as she forced herself to face up to the truth for the first time. 'Just awful. I said that it wasn't a good night to be out driving...but he wouldn't listen... He just wouldn't *listen*!'

Guy nodded as the strands of her story began to be woven together, beginning to make some sense of her guilt.

'I told him to be sure and ring me when he got to the pub, only the phone call didn't come, and I wasn't sure if he was sulking because he was angry with me...and...'

'And?' His voice was soft. Too soft. How could you resist a voice that soft?

'And when I rang the pub...' Sabrina bit her lip '...they said they hadn't seen him. So I thought he must have changed his mind about going there, never dreaming...never dreaming—'

'Never dreaming that the inconceivable had happened,' he said carefully, 'and that he'd never be coming back again?'

His words were edged with anger, and an emotion it took her a moment or two to recognise. Pain. 'That's right,' she agreed slowly.

'So you think that you should have stopped him from driving that night?'

'Of course I should have stopped him!' she shot back bitterly, but Guy shook his dark head.

'Don't you know that we can't govern other people's lives?' he demanded quietly. 'Or decide their destiny. You could have stopped him from going, but how do you know that he wouldn't have been hit by a bus on his way to work the next day? Maybe,' he added, with slow deliberation, 'maybe it was just his time.'

Her lips froze. 'His time?'

'To die.' His mouth hardened.

'Fate,' she elaborated painfully. 'That's fate.'

'Yeah, fate.'

She stared straight into the burning silver gaze, dazzled by it. 'You honestly believe that?' she whispered, and he gave a hollow kind of laugh.

'Sometimes it's easier to think of it that way.' He shrugged. 'Easier for the living to let go and carry on. And you have to let go, Sabrina, you *have* to—you must realise that. Don't you?'

'But I feel so guilty!'

'Because he's dead and you're alive?'

His perception took her breath away. 'Yes.'

He gave a brittle smile. 'But nothing can change that,

Sabrina. Nothing can bring him back. You owe it to yourself to let go. And to Michael.'

'Yes.' She sighed with a kind of surrender made all the easier by that luminous look of understanding. 'Yes.'

He watched as the thready breath made her lips tremble, he saw her wide-eyed look of trust, and he knew what she wanted and needed more than anything else at the moment. Pure animal comfort. Even if doing it would half kill him.

He drew her into the circle of his arms and hugged her tightly against his chest, the wetness of her tears warming his skin through his shirt. Her breasts were soft and pointed and her hair was full of the scent of lilac, and it took every bit of his self-control to dampen down his instinctive desire as he smoothed the bright strands down with a distracted hand.

'It's going to be OK,' he muttered, and prayed for his body not to react to her proximity. 'I promise you.'

Through her tears it occurred to Sabrina that his kindness and understanding were just two more facets of a complex personality which perplexed and intrigued her more with each day that passed. And that simply wasn't on the agenda. Her stay here was only temporary, she reminded herself as more tears spilled onto his shirt.

Guy let her cry until her sobs became dry and shuddering, and then he went and made her some hot chocolate, sitting in front of her like a determined nurse while she drank it.

He thought how unselfconsciously provocative her movements were. Thought that she shouldn't look that sexy with eyes bright red from crying and hair which was matted by those tears. But sexy she looked. Extremely sexy.

'So.' He sat back on his heels. 'Are you going to let it go now, Sabrina?'

She couldn't have said no, even if she'd wanted to, not

with that silver gaze compelling her to start living her life again. 'Yes,' she said slowly. 'I am.'

'Good.' He smiled. 'And are you going to let me take you out for dinner next week?'

She forced herself to remember that the question wasn't as warmly intimate as it sounded. 'Sure,' she said lightly. 'Is this the client dinner?'

'That's right,' he agreed. 'I have a Middle-Eastern potentate I've just bought a picture for. How would you like to have dinner with Prince Khalim?'

'*Prince* Khalim?' She gulped. 'Just how many princes do you know, Guy?'

He smiled. 'Khalim is my oldest friend. I've known him since schooldays—it was through him I got most of my contacts.'

'But, Guy—'

'Don't worry about it,' he soothed. 'You'll like him—a little old-fashioned perhaps, but he's a nice guy.'

with that sultry gaze and getting her to and fro from her job again.

'Good?' he smiled. 'And are you ready to let me take you out for dinner?'

She forced herself to remember the question with

## CHAPTER ELEVEN

FOR the next week, Sabrina was in a complete state of nerves. What on earth did you wear if you were going out for dinner with a *prince*?

She rang her mother and explained her predicament.

'Good heavens,' said her mother faintly. 'A *prince*? You'll never want to come home to Salisbury at this rate!'

Sabrina winced at how her mother had unerringly hit on the truth. She couldn't imagine wanting to either, but that had everything to do with Guy and nothing whatsoever to do with a Middle-Eastern potentate.

'What do I *wear*, Mum?' she repeated patiently.

'You've got lots of lovely clothes! Just be yourself,' said her mother. 'My goodness—wait until the neighbours hear about *this*!'

'Well, I don't want you to tell them,' said Sabrina stubbornly. Because however much she wished otherwise, one day soon she was going to have to go back and live at home, and she would do herself no favours whatsoever if she arrived with Guy Masters's magic dust still clinging to her skin.

She even tried to quiz Guy about the correct dress code one evening when he arrived home even later than usual and had been in a snarling temper. She produced a huge tureen of soup, and he stared down at the steaming bowlful and suddenly went very quiet.

'You don't like home-made soup?' she asked nervously.

Guy looked up. The soup looked perfect. Damn it—*she* looked perfect, standing there in a pair of white jeans and a white T-shirt, with her bright hair caught back in a po-nytail.

'Haven't had a lot of experience of it,' he said shortly. 'My mother used to open a can.'

Sabrina pushed some cheese across the table towards him. 'Wasn't she keen on cooking, then?'

It was an such an artless question that Guy found himself uncharacteristically answering it. 'Not particularly. And we were always...moving,' he said slowly. 'So a lot of her time was taken up with settling into new places.'

'You make it sound quite nomadic, Guy.'

'Do I? I suppose it was when you compare it with living in one place all your life.'

'Like me, you mean?'

He shrugged. 'Well, you did, didn't you?'

'Yes,' she said carefully, as some warning light in his eyes told her to go back to the safer subject of cooking, rather than the potential minefield of childhood.

She sawed through a crusty loaf and handed him a huge chunk of it. 'My mother was so busy going out to work that she never had time to cook properly, except at week-ends.'

He nodded, seeing the sudden, defensive set of her face. Despite his reservations, he found himself asking, 'How old were you when your father left?'

'Eight.' She pulled a face. 'He fell in love with my mum's "best" friend.'

He winced. 'That must have been tough.'

'Yes.' She stared down at the soup without really seeing it. 'For a while it was dreadful.' She looked up and gave him a bright smile. 'But time heals, doesn't it? Corny, but true.'

'Yeah, but you always get left with a scar.' He shrugged, but he shook his head at the silent question in her eyes. 'Tell me more.'

'Just I always vowed that when I grew up I would learn how to cook properly.'

Unexpectedly, he found the thought of Sabrina as a little girl exquisitely touching. He sipped the soup. 'Well, you achieved it with honours,' he murmured.

She glowed with pleasure. 'Guy?'

'Mmm?'

'You know this dinner on Saturday night—'

He put his spoon down. 'Damn!'

'It's been cancelled?' she asked hopefully.

He shook his head. 'Nope—but I haven't organised anything and I'm in Paris all day tomorrow. You'll have to book the restaurant, Sabrina.'

'Like *Where*? I don't really know London at all!'

He reeled off a list of London's most famous eating places and Sabrina shook her head doubtfully.

'We'll never get a table at any of those places *this* late!'

He gave a small smile. 'Just try mentioning my name.'

From anyone else it would have sounded outrageously arrogant—from Guy it just sounded supremely confident.

'And what on earth can I *wear*?' she wailed.

'Wear what you want.' He shrugged. 'You always look pretty good to me.'

She had received better compliments in her life, but none had she embraced as warmly as Guy's careless words and she had to force herself to suppress the guilt. She *was* letting go, and starting to live again—and there was nothing unacceptable about enjoying a compliment.

It still didn't solve the problem of what to wear, of course.

Guy left at the crack of dawn the following morning. Sabrina heard him moving around the flat and for once came, yawning, out into the hall to say goodbye to him.

His hand tightened around the handle of his briefcase as he saw her hair in all its tousled disarray tumbling down over her shoulders. Was she trying to play the siren? he wondered distractedly. But that was just the thing—he honestly didn't think she *was*.

'Have you remembered your passport?'

'Sabrina!' he exploded. 'I've been flying to Paris at least once a month for the last I don't know how long! How the hell do you think I managed before you came into my life?' It had been a calm, ordered time which was slowly but surely fading from his memory, the end of which had seemed to coincide with him urging her to let her guilt and her sorrow go. He had only himself to blame, and yet he hadn't realised how familiar it could feel, living with a woman—even if you *weren't* having sex with her. He winced. Why remind himself of *that*?

'Send me a postcard.' Sabrina smiled.

'I won't have time,' he said tightly, because he was having to fight the terrible urge to kiss her goodbye—as if she were his *wife* or something. His smile tasted like acid on his mouth. 'And don't forget to book the damned restaurant!'

'I won't forget.' She stood at the front door until he'd disappeared out of sight, praying that he would turn round and give her that rare and brilliant smile. But he didn't.

Sabrina felt more than a little intimidated at the thought of booking a meal at a place she had only ever read about in magazines. Wouldn't even her best dress look out of place in a venue as upmarket as that? And, when she thought about it, wouldn't Prince Khalim be bored rigid with going to fancy restaurants, and Guy, too, for that matter? Wouldn't they rather try something a little *different*?

She spent her lunch-hour scouring the restaurant section of the capital's biggest glossy magazine, and eventually found what she'd half thought she'd been looking for. She picked up the phone and booked it.

But Guy was delayed in Paris. He phoned that night.

'This deal is taking longer than I thought,' he said, and she could hear the sounds of people in the background. 'I may even have to stay over for a few days.'

'A few *days*?'

'You'll be OK on your own, won't you?'

Sabrina pulled a face. She couldn't be missing him *already*, could she? 'Yes, of course I will.'

'Just lock up carefully.' There was a pause. 'Ring Tom Roberts if you need anything. Actually, I'll ring him—get him to keep an eye on you.'

'I don't need anyone to keep an eye on me! You make me sound helpless!' she objected, and could hear the smile in his response.

'Not helpless, Sabrina. Maybe just a little vulnerable at the moment.' And make damned sure you remember that, he thought grimly as he hung up before tapping out Tom's number.

Guy arrived back from Paris on Saturday morning, feeling all frazzled and frayed around the edges as he walked into the kitchen to a delicious smell of coffee. Sabrina was already dressed, busy buttering a slice of toast. He paused for a moment which felt dangerous. Because his kitchen had never felt more of a home than it did at that moment.

He'd missed her, he realised with a sudden sense of shock.

'Hi,' he said softly.

Sabrina turned round slowly, trying to compose her face, making sure that every trace of leaping excitement had been eradicated from her features. She smiled instead. 'Welcome home! How was your trip? Would you like some coffee?'

He wanted something a lot more fundamental than coffee, but he nodded his head, sat down at the table and took the mug of coffee she slid towards him.

'You're up early,' he commented.

'I'm working today, remember?'

He frowned. Had it really been three weeks since the last time she'd been in the shop on Saturday morning? 'Yeah.' He sighed. He'd been almost tempted to take the day off himself, and to ask her whether she wanted to go to a gallery with him, but if she was working… 'I guess I might as well go in myself.' He yawned.

Sabrina fixed him with a stern look. 'Oh, for goodness' sake, Guy! You've only just got back from Paris. Give yourself a break!'

He glared at her. 'I've managed to get along just fine for the last thirty-two years without anyone telling me how to live my life, if it's all the same to you, Sabrina.' He paused. 'Did you book the restaurant?'

'I did,' she said steadily, without missing a beat.

'Which one?'

Her bright smiled didn't falter. 'It's a surprise!'

'A surprise?'

She wondered what had caused that sudden hardening of his voice. 'You don't like surprises?'

'No,' he clipped out, and then saw her crestfallen face and relented. It was unpredictability he shied away from. She wasn't to know that surprises made him feel as though the control which was so fundamental to him could be in danger of slipping away. Loosen up, he told himself—just as he'd told her to. He smiled. 'It had better be a good one.'

'Oh, I think it will be.'

'We're picking Khalim up from his hotel at eight.'

She nodded, trying to be helpful. 'So shall I order us a car, too?'

'Yes,' he murmured, wondering why he got the distinct impression that the balance of power had somehow shifted in this relationship without him really noticing. He'd wanted her to try and let the past go, but he hadn't expected such an enchanting switch into sexy and sassy and bossy mode. It was much too irresistible a transformation. 'Thanks,' he added heavily.

Sabrina spent hours in the bathroom getting ready, comfortable in the knowledge that she wouldn't be holding Guy up. Thank heavens there were three, she thought, remembering her initial shock at discovering that one flat had three bathrooms all to itself. Back in Salisbury her mother would have been beating the door down by now.

In the spare room, she pulled out the hanger on which hung the dress she'd bought after work yesterday, and she looked at it with eager eyes. It was a dream—easily the most grown-up and sophisticated thing she had ever owned—but nothing less would do, not for a prince!

It was in deepest violet velvet and it fell to just above the knee, with long, fitted sleeves. In fact, the whole dress accentuated every curve of her body and the rich, vibrant colour contrasted deeply with her red-gold hair. It was a simple dress, possibly a little *too* simple, which was why she'd bought diamanté earrings and an ornate and glittering necklace to go with it.

She stepped back to look at herself in the mirror and gave a nod of satisfaction. The diamanté necklace and earrings sparkled and spangled in the light. She looked good! Maybe the best she had ever looked—and there was an added sparkle to her eyes and a soft flush to her cheeks.

Guy was standing by the window in the sitting room, doing up his cuff-links, and he looked up as she made her entrance, then froze.

Sabrina, who had been watching him expectantly, saw the sudden stiffening of his body, the swift hard gleam in his eyes, and her heart sank.

'You don't think it's suitable?'

A pulse hammered at his temple. 'Don't be so bloody naïve, Sabrina! Of course it's suitable—' He'd never seen anything more suitable in his life—and the thing it was most suitable for was being ripped off her body... He groaned and tried to pay a gracious compliment. 'It's lovely,' he finished lamely.

'Oh. Right.' She screwed her nose up. 'You don't think it's too over the top?'

'*No*, I don't!' He drew a deep breath. 'And I think we've just about exhausted the subject of what you're wearing. Now, where the hell is this bloody car?'

Sabrina hoped that he was going to moderate his language a little, especially in front of Prince Khalim, but now didn't seem a very good time to say so, especially since at that moment the doorbell rang, and the chauffeur was standing there, telling them that their car was ready. She picked up the same diaphanous silver wrap she'd worn in Venice and turned to Guy.

'Ready?' she asked, thinking that she'd never seen him in formal black tie regalia before, and just how darkly imposing and broad-shouldered it made him appear.

'And waiting,' he said, in a grim kind of voice.

Outside stood a long, gleaming, black car which made the limousine he'd hired in Salisbury look like an ancient old banger. Sabrina felt like a film star as she climbed inside.

But as they were whisked towards the West End Guy seemed to want to avoid all her attempts at conversation, and Sabrina forced herself to look out of the window, trying to appear interested in the sights as they sped by, wondering why he was sitting in such stony silence.

All he could think about was how much he wanted to kiss her, and it was driving him out of his mind. Since when had *kissing* been his number-one priority?

The car slid to a halt in front of the Granchester Hotel, which was situated right opposite Hyde Park and where a uniformed doorman immediately sprang to attention.

'I'd better go inside and tell him we're here,' said Guy, still in that same, heavy voice.

But at that moment there was some sort of commotion and several burly men in suits emerged from the hotel entrance and stood, looking this way and that.

'That's his security,' said Guy, seeing her expression of bemusement. 'They may want to check the restaurant out so your little "surprise" may have to be unmasked, Sabrina, dearest.'

In the dim light of the early evening, Sabrina blanched. Maybe she had misjudged the whole situation completely, but by then it was too late to do anything about it because the men in suits had all stood up straight to attention. And the most striking man she had ever seen in her life came gliding out of the hotel.

It wasn't just the fact that he was tall—although Guy was actually taller by about a head. Or that he was wearing a long, silky kind of robe which was a cross between white and gold and hinted at a hard body beneath. Or that his hair was darker than the night—much blacker than Guy's—and his skin the deep golden colour of some ancient and lovingly polished piece of wood. Or that his eyes were as black as onyx itself—curiously deep, all-seeing eyes which were as emotionless and as cold as any she had ever seen.

For he was all those things, and more, thought Sabrina. He was a prince—and not just by title. He oozed it from every autocratic pore of his body.

His nose was a cruel, hard curve, and so was his mouth, and something about his whole rather rich and haughty demeanour made Sabrina feel slightly panicky with nerves as she recalled the restaurant booking she'd made. What had she *done*?

As Guy opened the door he felt Sabrina shiver beside him, and he glanced down at her, his mouth tightening. So the old knockout Khalim effect was having its usual reaction, he thought cynically.

'Don't worry, he likes blondes,' he told her cryptically. 'So you should be on to a winner!'

'But I'm a strawberry-blonde!' she objected, stung by that critical note in his voice. 'That's different.'

'And strawberries are rich and luscious,' Guy answered softly. 'Be careful, Sabrina—he eats women like you for breakfast.'

Sabrina glared at his back as he stepped from the car and the two men greeted each other like the old friends they were.

'Guy!' said Khalim, the hard lips curving into a smile.

Guy jerked his head in the direction of the suits. 'Are you bringing this lot with you?'

Khalim glanced a flickering look at the back of the car, where Sabrina was sitting frozen with nerves. The black eyes narrowed.

'They will follow behind us,' he said, 'but they will sit outside in the car. They shall not bother us while we are eating.' His voice softened as another dark, enigmatic glance was directed at the car. 'And who do you have sitting and waiting so beautifully for us, Guy?'

Guy felt an unwelcome flicker of irritation. This was Khalim, Khalim whom he had known since school—when they'd forged an instant friendship after Guy had beaten him at chess. Khalim had never been beaten by anyone before—but, then, as Guy had coolly pointed out, he'd been brought up in an environment where letting Khalim win was paramount.

The two boys had fallen with fists on one another, and had had to be pulled apart—both snarling and glaring like young tiger cubs. And then one of them—they'd each taken the credit afterwards—had started laughing, and the laughter had been contagious and had created a bond which had never been broken down the years.

Khalim's father had given Guy his first big break, and Guy had never forgotten that.

So why did he now feel like the small boy who'd wanted to pulverise his schoolmate?

'This is Sabrina,' said Guy shortly.

He pulled open the car door and Khalim slid inside next to Sabrina, the silken fabric of his robe whispering and clinging to the lean definition of his muscular legs. 'Sabrina Cooper.'

'And Sabrina is your...?' Khalim paused delicately, as if searching for the right word.

'Friend,' said Guy instantly, because in that instant no other word seemed to do. 'She's staying in my flat for a few weeks.'

'Indeed?' murmured Khalim.

Sabrina felt the slow thudding of disappointment. Every word Guy had said was true—but, oh, if he'd wanted to emphasise that their love affair was dead, that her role in his life only transitory, then he couldn't have done it more succinctly. Or more cruelly.

'That's right,' she said staunchly, and attempted to echo his casual tone. 'I'm just passing through.'

'Indeed?' murmured Khalim again. Black eyes glinted as he raised her hand and lightly brushed his lips against the fingertips. 'Khalim,' he purred. 'And I am charmed.'

It was difficult not to be charmed herself by such quaintly old-fashioned manners. And the sight of Guy glowering from the other side of the car had her smiling back at the Prince.

'I've booked the restaurant for tonight,' she babbled. 'I do hope I've made the right choice.'

The curved smile edged upwards. 'Water and bread can

be sustenance enough,' said Khalim softly, 'when the company is this spectacular.'

Guy turned his head to look out of the window, thinking that he just might be sick. He'd heard Khalim's chat-up lines over the years—and as far as he knew—they had a one hundred per cent success rate. But this...this... *outrageous* flirting was really too much.

Sabrina had given the restaurant address to the driver when she'd made the phone booking for the car, but as it negotiated its way through Notting Hill and drew up outside a small, colourful café, her heart sank.

The signs, it had to be admitted, didn't look very promising. There was a garish awning outside, beneath which the sign read, THE PIE SHOP.

Guy's eyes narrowed incredulously. 'Just what *is* this place, Sabrina?'

'It got a very good review in the papers,' she defended, determined not to flinch beneath the quiet look of fury in his eyes. 'And I thought it would be...different.'

'It is certainly different,' said Khalim, his voice tilting with amusement. 'Come, let us go and see what delights The Pie Shop has to offer.

It was the kind of place which employed out-of-work actresses as waitresses—so at least the glamour quotient was high. But Khalim didn't seem at all interested in the nubile specimens who ushered them inside. In fact, his attention seemed to be all on Sabrina.

Almost worryingly so, she told herself as they were given a table in the corner.

There were no menus, just a huge blackboard with the dishes of the day printed on it in chalk.

'I'm surprised there isn't sawdust on the floor,' said Guy acidly, but Khalim was gazing around him with the air of a man who had stepped into a different world.

'No, but it is charming,' he murmured. 'Quite charming.

And the smell of the food delicious. Every summer my mother used to take me and my sisters into the mountains, and we would eat a meal with an old man who had spent his life caring for the goats and living in a simple dwelling. This place reminds me of that.'

Oh, *great*, thought Guy. He frosted a look at Sabrina across the table. 'Khalim hasn't eaten red meat for years.' He gave a pointed stare at the dish of the day—shepherd's pie. 'Any suggestions, Sabrina?'

She thought that she'd never seen him quite this grumpy before, but it occurred to her that if he hadn't wanted her to come along, then he shouldn't have asked her. 'How about fish pie?' she suggested brightly.

'Fish *pie*,' echoed Khalim, as if she'd just proposed a lavish banquet. 'Do you know—I haven't eaten fish pie since we were at school. Do you remember, Guy? Always on Fridays.' And he gave a wistful smile, which briefly softened his hard, proud face.

How did she *do* it, wondered Guy distractedly. How had she unerringly hit on the one dish which would produce a rare state of nostalgia in a man who'd very probably been offered every delicacy under the sun?

'Three fish pies,' he said to the waitress, and Sabrina, who'd been about to order the shepherd's pie, hastily shut her mouth. It might be considered bad manners to eat meat in front of the Prince.

It wasn't the easiest meal she had ever sat through, mainly because Guy would hardly meet her eye, just chatted to Khalim about the paintings he'd seen recently in Paris.

Khalim listened and ate his meal slowly and with evident pleasure. Occasionally he would turn to Sabrina and fix her with that hard, black stare as he asked her about her work in the bookshop as if it were the single most fascinating subject in the world.

And Sabrina smiled and tried to look attentive, while miserably ploughing her way through the fish pie.

After she'd pushed her plate away, Khalim leaned forward, his fingertips brushing against the bright glitter of her necklace.

'Who bought you these diamonds, my beauty?' he murmured.

Sabrina smiled. 'Oh, they're not real!'

'Really?' Khalim brushed one of the gems thoughtfully. 'Then it must be your skin which enhances them—for they look absolutely priceless.'

What Khalim didn't know about diamonds could be written on the back of a postage stamp, and Guy watched with increasing fury as the Prince's dark, elegant fingers contrasted against her milk-white skin.

'Shall we skip pudding?' he demanded.

They ordered coffee instead, and Guy was just paying the bill when Khalim lightly placed his hand on Sabrina's wrist.

'I'm in England for another couple of weeks,' he mused. 'Perhaps you would have dinner with me some night?'

Sabrina looked over at Guy, unsure of how you went about saying to a prince that it was a terribly sweet offer but that she was fast falling in love with someone else, thank you.

*In love?* Her cheeks grew hot, and the pounding in her heart increased. What in heaven's name was she thinking of? She couldn't be falling in love. She *couldn't*. It was too soon after Michael—much too soon.

She glanced over at the object of her affections, who was chatting to the waitress and giving her the benefit of the sunniest smile she'd seen all evening.

'Sabrina?' prompted Khalim softly.

Well, all *right*, she thought furiously, and smiled back at him. 'That would be wonderful,' she agreed shyly.

# CHAPTER TWELVE

GUY maintained a simmering silence all the way home, even after they'd left Khalim back at his hotel and the chauffeur had dropped them back at the flat.

In fact, he waited until he'd slammed the front door behind them. He didn't have many neighbours, it was true, but the ones he did have had known him for years. And would probably have gone into extreme shock if they'd heard Guy Masters yelling at a woman, which was exactly what he felt like doing.

'Are you *mad*?' he demanded.

'And are *you* lacking in any social graces?' Sabrina returned hotly.

'You spent the whole night simpering up to Khalim!'

'Only because you could hardly bring yourself to say a civil word to me—and I was *not* simpering!'

He steadied his breath. Stay calm, he told himself. Stay calm. This wasn't like him at all. 'Do you have any idea of that man's reputation with women?'

Sabrina met his eyes with dignity. 'He seemed quite the gentleman—'

'*Quite the gentleman?*' he repeated faintly.

'Besides, I thought he was your friend.'

He heard the rebuke in her voice. 'He *is* my friend! He also has a legendary libido. Legendary. I can't believe that you'd be so naïve, Sabrina.' And he pictured the two of them together, and the black dagger of jealousy cut into him and sent the words spilling out before he could stop them. 'You weren't so naïve when...' But the words died as soon as he saw the look on her face.

142

'When what, Guy?' she asked coldly.

'Nothing.'

But she wasn't going to let this one rest. 'Oh, yes—
*something*,' she contradicted furiously. 'Perhaps you think
that if I go out with Khalim, I'll fall straight into bed with
him. That he will be able to seduce me with the same ease
as you did.'

He saw the hurt which clouded her ice-blue eyes and his
mouth tightened. 'That's not what I said.'

'It's what you meant, though, isn't it? Well, *damn* you,
Guy Masters, if that's your opinion of me, then there's no
point me saying any more, is there? You obviously think
I'm a tramp!' And she stalked off down to her bedroom,
trembling with rage and distress.

He watched her go, fighting down the urge to run after
her because he knew what the only outcome would be if
he confronted her when emotions were running so high.
God, he'd barely been able to watch Khalim coming on to
her all night. And yet with his jealousy he'd offended her.
Deeply.

But the time for reconciliation would be in the cold, clear
light of logical thinking, not now—not when he was aching
for her so badly that if he got within touching distance of
her he would just want to haul her into his arms and crush
his mouth down on hers and... Stifling a groan, he went
off to take a much-needed shower.

Sabrina spent a restless night and woke up remembering
the scene of the night before. And Guy's appalling insin-
uations. She turned onto her side and gazed sightlessly up
at the wall, wondering if those heated words should change
things.

She could leave and go back to Salisbury now. Today,
if she really wanted to. Maybe that was what a sane, sen-

sible person would do. The trouble was that she felt neither particularly sane nor particularly sensible. She wanted...

She turned onto her other side and stared at the exercise bike, which was now positioned underneath the window. What *did* she want?

Most of her wanted Guy, with a growing love she hardly dared to acknowledge—but what did Guy want?

Nothing, it would appear.

Oh, she suspected that he still felt desire for her—she wasn't *stupid*. She had seen that unmistakable darkening of his eyes, the sudden tension of his body when she'd been close to him sometimes. He certainly wasn't immune to her—but neither did he seem to want to do anything about it.

She sighed. Perhaps she should just be grateful that he was behaving like such a gentleman. Her mother *would* be pleased.

There was a rap on the door, and a voice called out softly, 'Sabrina? Are you awake?'

'I am now!' she replied acidly.

Behind the door, Guy smiled. 'I'm making breakfast.'

'What do you want—a medal?'

'Just your company.'

She pushed the duvet back and stepped out of bed. What was the point in sulking, and pretending she hated him? If she intended to stay—and she did—she couldn't behave like a petulant child simply because he'd lost his temper with her last night. 'You'll have to wait until I'm showered and dressed,' she said.

Guy gave another wry smile. The trouble was that he liked it when she started laying down the law. And it was novel enough to be very, very stimulating. 'Don't take too long.'

'Then go away and leave me to it.'

'Yes, Sabrina,' he murmured.

She appeared dressed and showered twenty minutes later, to find that he'd put a crisp white cloth on the dining-room table and there were freshly squeezed juice, warm croissants and different jams. And he was sitting, barefooted, in jeans and a T-shirt, reading a newspaper.

He looked up as she came in and their eyes met.

'I'm sorry,' he said, and forced himself to behave like a calm and rational human being instead of some kind of jealous monster. 'I had absolutely no right to talk to you like that. Whether or not you choose to go out with Khalim is entirely up to you.'

'You're absolutely right,' Sabrina agreed coolly as she sat down opposite him and picked up a napkin. 'It is.'

It was not the answer he'd been expecting. Or wanted. But he forced himself to smile. 'I'm going into the office for a couple of hours,' he said.

'But it's Sunday!' She pouted disapprovingly.

'Princess,' he said grimly, because much more of this and he really might lose his head. Or something even more dangerous. Like his heart. 'I just about know my days of the week!'

'You're going to burn out before you're forty,' she warned.

He drummed his fingers on the table. 'Lecture over now, is it, Sabrina?'

They spent the rest of that week being extremely polite to each other. And more than a little wary.

He was home earlier than usual on Thursday. Just as he'd been home earlier on Tuesday. Funny how the office suddenly seemed to have lost some of its old allure. He'd picked up a take-away on the way home, and they'd stood together, unpacking the foil containers, while Guy tried very hard not to be diverted by the sweet sheen of her hair.

'How about dinner tomorrow night?' he asked suddenly. Sabrina looked up, surprised that he was keen to repeat

the experience after what had happened last time. Unless…
'You mean, with you?'

'Yeah, and another client.'

Her heart fell, but she was damned if she would show it. 'Not Khalim?' she posed, wondering guiltily whether she ought to tell him that an exquisite orchid from the Prince had arrived by post yesterday. And it was hidden in all its scented beauty in the one place that Guy would never find it.

Her bedroom.

'No, not Khalim.' He spooned some rice onto his plate. 'Actually, it's a businessman who wants to buy a painting which has just come onto the market.' He shrugged. 'Even though he doesn't particularly like it.'

'Then why on earth is he buying it?'

'As an investment. And as a coup.' The ice-blue eyes were narrowed at him perceptively. She had a strange and infuriating habit of looking at him in that questioning way, and when she did he just couldn't seem to resist telling her what she wanted to know. 'He's a bit of an idiot, actually.'

Sabrina put the spoon down. 'And you want to give up your Friday night to have dinner with an idiot—and mine, too?'

'It's business.'

'Oh, yes—*business*.' She couldn't keep the derision out of her voice. 'Better not miss out, then, Guy—you really need that extra million bucks, don't you?'

Guy froze. He hadn't been the recipient of undiluted criticism for more years than he cared to remember, and even if it had more than a kernel of truth in it, it wasn't *her* damned place to give it to him. 'I take it that's a refusal?' he snapped, thinking that there wasn't a single other woman of his acquaintance who would have turned him down.

'Too right it is! I'd rather stay in and read my book, if you must know.'

'Fine,' he said tightly. 'Then do that.'

'I will!'

They had just sat down in a frosty silence to eat their meal when the telephone began to ring.

'You'd better get that, Guy,' said Sabrina sweetly. 'You virtually bit my head off the last time I answered it when you were here!'

And no wonder. He stood up. Ever since that day his mother had taken to ringing him at work and bombarding him with all kinds of questions about Sabrina. Where had they met, and what was she like? And the more he seemed to protest that she was nothing more than a girl who happened to be staying for a while, the less his mother seemed to believe him.

'You've never had a woman living with you before,' she'd pointed out.

'She's not living *with* me,' he'd explained tersely. 'Just living in the same flat. It's no big deal, Ma—people do it all the time these days.'

'Not someone like you,' his mother had said serenely. 'I know how you like to be in control.'

'So?'

'Well, as every year passes you become more and more eligible—'

'Ma,' he'd objected on a note of drawling humour.

'It's true. And an attractive young woman invading your space would normally have you running screaming in the opposite direction.'

'Who says she's attractive?' Guy had asked suspiciously.

'Well, *is* she?'

'Mmm,' he'd agreed, without thinking. 'She is. Very.'

His mother had sounded oddly triumphant. 'So when are we going to meet her? Your brother and I are itching with curiosity.'

'Then itch away. You are *not* going to meet her,' he'd

said patiently. Then, having heard his mother's offended silence, he'd sighed. 'Not just yet, anyway...'

He picked the phone up. 'Guy Masters.'

'Guy? Khalim here.'

'Khalim!' He forced enthusiasm into his voice. 'What can I do for you?'

'May I speak with Sabrina, please?' came the honey-smooth response. 'I was going to ask her out to dinner on Saturday.'

Resisting the urge to slam the phone down, Guy marched back into the dining room. 'It's Khalim on the phone,' he said accusingly. 'For *you*.'

Infuriatingly, Sabrina found herself thinking about the orchid, and felt the blood rush hotly into her cheeks. 'I wonder what he wants.'

'To ask you out for dinner.' He stared at the pink cheeks and wondered what had caused her to blush. 'But we've been invited out to a party on Saturday.'

'We?' she asked disbelievingly.

'Well, I have,' he admitted. 'But I'm sure that Jenna won't mind if I bring someone.'

Oh, sure. Sabrina could just imagine how much Jenna would like *her* there. 'Jenna doesn't like me, Guy—on the only two occasions I've met her, she's looked at me as though I was an insect she found squashed onto the sole of her shoe.'

'She's better with men than with women,' he observed.

Understatement of the year. Sabrina paused by the door, thinking that she was fed up with only being good enough for client dinners with idiots or as the unwanted guest at the party of a predatory woman who obviously wanted Guy for herself.

'Actually, I just might go out with Khalim,' she said. 'It could be rather fun.'

Guy could hear her on the phone to his friend, and his

pulse began to hammer. He pushed his barely touched plate of food away, and scowled. She could do what she damned well liked.

Inexplicably, Guy found himself cancelling the client dinner on Friday, and then spent the next evening prowling the sitting room like an edgy jungle cat as he waited for Khalim to arrive. He seethed when Sabrina breezed into the sitting room and he saw that she was wearing that same silky silvery grey dress she'd worn in Venice. The night he'd taken her to his bed.

It was on the tip of his tongue to ask her whether she intended an action replay with his friend, but some last vestige of sanity made him bite back the jealous words that he instinctively knew she would never forgive. Words that deep down he knew he didn't mean—so why the hell did he keep imagining the whole scenario, as if someone were running a film reel through his mind?

Sabrina felt slightly on edge, wondering if she was equipped to cope with a man who, as Guy had already said, ate women like her for breakfast.

Suddenly she wished that she hadn't been so proud, or so stupid. Fancy letting Guy go alone to a party where Jenna would no doubt be waiting to get her hooks in him. 'Aren't you going to be late, Guy?' she asked tentatively, and then almost recoiled from the anger in his eyes.

'Want me to get out from under your feet?' he asked silkily.

'Don't be so insulting!'

He picked up his jacket with a careless finger. 'Just be careful, huh? You've got the number of my mobile, haven't you?'

'Why, do you think he's about to drag me off to his palace with him to make mad love to me all night?' she asked sarcastically.

'I wouldn't blame him if he did,' he drawled. He looked

at the silver-grey fabric, which clung so enticingly to the slender curves of her body, and swallowed. If Khalim attempted to do that then as one man to another he would completely be able to understand it. 'But just remember this, Sabrina—he'll never marry an Englishwoman. His destiny has been mapped out for him since birth.'

'I'm not looking for a husband!' she snapped.

'Good.' He gave the ghost of a smile. 'Have a good time.'

'What, after *that* little pep-talk?' she asked acidly.

After Guy had gone, she felt like ringing up Khalim to cancel—but, apart from the fact that she didn't have a number for him—even Sabrina realised that such a loss of face would be intolerable to a man like the Prince.

Even so, she felt as if the executioner's axe was about to fall while she waited for the doorbell to ring.

Guy walked into the party and wished he could walk straight out again. He narrowed his eyes against the mêlée. Too many people, too much noise, too much smoke, and the music was *hellish*.

'Hello, Guy,' came a low, husky voice by his side, and he turned round to see Jenna, an expression he didn't quite recognise making her lovely face look a little less lovely than usual.

'Hi,' he said, thinking how overly jovial he sounded. He handed her a slim, silver-wrapped present. 'Happy birthday!'

'For me?' she said coyly. 'What is it?'

The question irritated him far more than it had any right to. 'Why not open it and see?'

Jenna's perfectly painted fingernails greedily ripped open the paper. 'Oh,' she said slowly. 'A book.'

She said it, thought Guy wryly, as though he'd just given her a serpent.

'Apparently, if you only read one book for the rest of

your life, this is the one. It's up for a prize, and most people in the industry think it's just going to walk away with it.' He was, he realised, repeating Sabrina's enthusiastic praise almost word for word. She had recommended that he read it himself, and maybe he would. Maybe he would.

'Oh,' Jenna said.

The blinkers seemed to drop from his eyes as he surveyed Jenna's look of bemusement. It was going to be, he realised sadly, completely wasted on her. 'Hope you like it,' he finished lamely, and wondered just how long he could stay at this party without looking boorish.

'I'm sure I will!' Jenna's green eyes slanted from side to side. 'On your own?' she quizzed softly.

Something in her tone made his hackles rise. 'Obviously.'

Jenna shrugged. 'Nothing obvious about it at all—I'm suprised you haven't brought your new *flatmate* with you.'

Guy stared at her. Funny how you could know someone for years and years, and a remark which should have been completely inoffensive should suddenly sound like the most intolerable intrusion. His grey eyes gleamed. 'And why should that surprise you, Jenna?'

'Well…' Jenna drank some champagne and left some of the liquid to gleam provocatively on her lips. 'You know what people have been saying, don't you?'

'No, I don't. Why don't you tell me?' he suggested evenly.

Jenna shrugged. 'Oh, just that she's not your flatmate at all—but your lover.' She gave a shrill little laugh. 'As if!'

Some dark kind of explosion seemed to happen inside his head. 'You'd find that such a bizarre scenario, would you?' he asked quietly.

'Well…' Jenna shrugged, seemingly oblivious to the dangerous quality in his tone. 'I think that most people would, don't you? You're…' She gave a foolish, beaming smile, like someone who had decided to bet all their money on an outsider.

'Hmm? What am I?'

'You're...well, you're everything that most women would ever want, I suppose,' she stumbled. 'And she's...'

Guy froze. 'She's what?'

'Well, I'm sure she's very *nice*,' said Jenna insincerely. 'But she's just a small-town girl who works in a *bookshop*, isn't she?'

'As opposed to a small-minded girl who lives off her daddy's trust fund?'

Jenna stared at him. 'Guy!' she protested. 'That was completely uncalled for!'

His grey eyes were as cold as ice. 'What right do you think you have to criticise a sweet, beautiful woman who actually works hard for her living? Who has seen tragedy and looked it in the face, and managed to come to terms with it?'

'I didn't know anything about that!'

'You don't know anything about anything!' he snapped. 'Not about anything that really matters! Forgive me if I don't stay, Jenna, but I have something waiting for me at home!'

Or someone.

Except that he didn't—and why would he expect to? All he'd offered Sabrina had been some lousy dinner with a man he himself had admitted was a fool. And the only additional carrot he'd dangled in front of her had been a trip to the party of a woman who looked down her nose at her.

Was this what his life had become? Some kind of extravagant but superficial game? Going to all the right places but with all the wrong people—and for the wrong reasons, too?

And Sabrina was now out with Khalim—a man he liked and respected, but a man who was a veritable tiger where women were concerned. He had seen for himself that Khalim had been capitivated by Sabrina's easy, uncomplicated charm—just as he had been. He'd also said that Khalim would never marry an Englishwoman—but what if Sabrina's golden bright beauty was the exception to the rule? Khalim was used to getting whatever he wanted in life. Wouldn't he move heaven and earth to possess a woman if she'd touched his heart in a way that no one else had?

He drove like fury back to the flat, but it was, as he'd fully expected, empty.

He'd never spent a longer evening in his life—bar the one where he'd sat with his mother and waited for news which they'd both known in their hearts would be the worst possible news.

He tried reading, but that was useless, and he hated the television with a passion. He realised that he hadn't eaten, but couldn't face preparing any food. Or even eating some of Sabrina's carefully packed leftovers which sat at the back of the fridge. And the sight of her slavish economising made him want to hit something.

Or someone.

Guy forced himself to face the fact that she might not come home at all. That Khalim might now be making love to her with all the skill acquired from having had women offer themselves to him since he'd been barely out of his teens.

And if that *was* the case, then he must force himself to act like a rational man. He had no right to show temper or outrage. They weren't committing any crime. He didn't own her.

He glanced down at his watch. Where the hell *was* she?

He had just sprawled down on the sofa, a glass of wine in front of him, when he heard the sound of a key in the front door. He rose to his feet, but stood right where he was and waited. Because he knew that he might have to face the fact that Sabrina was not alone.

## CHAPTER THIRTEEN

SABRINA walked into the sitting room to find Guy standing there, as motionless as if he'd been carved from some beautiful dark and golden stone. His eyes were the only animated part of his body, and they swept over her in a glittering and hectic question.

'Is Khalim with you?'

She shook her head. 'No. He's just driven off.'

Guy expelled a quiet breath of relief, but he didn't move. He had rushed in once before. This time it had to be different. He gestured towards the bottle of claret which stood on the table. 'Would you like some wine?'

It had been an emotional evening. She had drunk mineral water and jasmine tea, but right then she needed a drink. 'I'd love one.'

He poured her a glass and put it down on one of the small tables, keeping his voice deliberately casual. 'So. Good evening, was it?'

Sabrina dropped her shawl over the back of one of the chairs and went to sit down on one of the sofas. It hadn't been the evening she'd been expecting. But then she hadn't expected to find herself weeping quietly on Khalim's shoulder and telling him that she was in love with Guy—and that if he ever said anything to Guy about it, she would never forgive him.

And Khalim, still slightly shell-shocked from the first rejection he had ever encountered, had given a rueful smile and smoothed a tear-soaked strand of hair away from her cheek with a gentle finger.

'You think I would risk you not forgiving me?' he'd

mused. 'You know, Guy is a strong man, not a stupid man—and he is behaving like one if he ignores this most precious gift which is his for the taking.'

Sabrina had bitten nervously at her lip. How could she possibly tell Khalim the truth? That she'd fallen into his friend's arms in Venice with such indecent haste that he probably had no respect left for her.

'He's not interested in me that way,' she'd told him stolidly. 'Not any more. I know he's not.'

'Then for the first time in my life I must question his judgement,' Khalim had replied in a hard, cold voice.

'And anyway,' she'd said, in a small voice, 'even if he was, I don't think I could bear to make myself that vulnerable again. If you love someone, then losing them is just unbearable.'

His dark eyes had narrowed. 'Explain,' he'd ordered quietly. And she'd told him all about Michael and he'd listened thoughtfully.

'So you see,' she'd finished, 'it's much too soon for me to fall in love with someone else—it does a disservice to Michael's memory.'

The hard lips had curved briefly into a smile. 'But love has no respect for convention, Sabrina,' he had sighed.

And from that moment on he had behaved almost as though she was sick, and in a way maybe she was. For the pain in her heart was real enough, surely? As real as the sharp pierce of longing which ripped right through her whenever she thought of Guy.

Khalim had made her eat a little something, and told her something of his homeland. His voice had lulled her and soothed her, and his softly accented descriptions of his upbringing had transported her to another world.

Just as Guy had transported her to another world.

But it wasn't her world.

'It was certainly different,' she said to Guy, as she remembered.

He forced himself to keep the jealous monster at bay. 'Oh?'

She sat down, picked up her glass and sipped at it gratefully, acutely aware of the glittering grey gaze which held her fast in its dazzle. She thought that he looked almost strained tonight, with a strange kind of restlessness about him.

'How was Jenna's party?'

'Boring as hell.'

'Really?'

'Really. But I don't want to talk about Jenna's party. I'm much more interested in your evening.'

'Oh, Khalim had hired a private room in the most amazing restaurant you've ever seen,' she said, still slightly reeling from the experience. 'Imagine—a whole room to ourselves!'

Behind the hard line of his mouth Guy gritted his teeth. Just a taste of Khalim's average over-the-top seduction technique. 'How very impressive,' he said steadily.

He really *did* seem to be tense, as if he was hanging onto his self-control with difficulty, and Sabrina stared at him, willing her heart not to wrench, but it was hopeless. Every time she looked at him she felt nothing but an unbearable sense of longing.

'It was. Very,' she said simply. No need to tell him that she'd barely eaten a thing, or that the spectacular surroundings hadn't registered. She might as well have been sitting in some scruffy old café for all that she would have noticed—because Guy hadn't been there. And the world was just not the same place when Guy wasn't there.

'And are you going to see him again?'

Something in the harshness of the question made her go

very still, and she gazed up into the hard contours of his face. 'And if I am?'

There was a dangerous pause. 'I don't like it.'

'*You* don't like it?' Sabrina stared at him. She thought about his rage when she'd told him she was going to accept Khalim's offer of a date. If she thought about it rationally, all the facts added up to jealousy. So, was Guy jealous of Khalim and, if so, why, when he had shown no signs of wanting her for himself? 'Why not?'

'Why do you think?' he snapped. 'Because it's doing my head in to think that he wants you when I want you so badly for myself.'

Joy mingled with disbelief. '*You*...want me?' she repeated, her voice trembling.

'Of course I want you! Haven't I wanted you ever since I made the foolish suggestion that you come and live here?'

'Why was it foolish?' she breathed.

He knew that now was not the time for his habitual evasion. 'Maybe I was just fooling myself into thinking that what happened in Venice was a reckless one-off.' Hadn't part of him secretly hoped it had been? He shook his head. 'But my feelings for you haven't changed.'

Sabrina stared at him. He'd used the word 'feelings', but she suspected that he really meant desire. But, however he chose to phrase it, it didn't really matter—because nothing could change the way she felt about him. Nothing.

'Haven't they?' she whispered.

'Not a bit.'

Guy watched her eyes darken involuntarily as their eyes locked, and saw the soft tremble of her lips. And suddenly he knew that neither logic nor reason could stop what he was about to do.

With a hand that wasn't quite steady he put his glass down on the table, walked over to the sofa and stood looking down at her. He saw the sudden parting of her lips as she read the answering hunger in his eyes.

'Guy?' she said breathlessly.

'Sabrina?' came the soft mocking response. 'Do you think we've played the waiting game for long enough?'

She could barely get the single word out. 'Y-yes.'

He held his hand out to her and she took it. In an instant she was in his arms, and his eyes were hard and bright and hungry as he brought his lips down to kiss her.

And just that first heady contact set her on fire. Blazing. With a tiny moan, she coiled her arms around his neck like a snake and he pulled her hard into his body so that their hips melded, and she could feel the hard, powerful jut of him throught the fine linen of his trousers.

He kissed her with a frustration that went bone-deep, and Guy found himself lost in the sweetness of her mouth, as if he could never get enough of plundering its honeyed moistness. He pulled her even closer, feeling the tips of her nipples as they strained against the sheer, silky fabric of her dress.

With an effort he pulled his lips away from hers, and she made a murmured little protest as he looked down at her, his eyes glittering black, opaque with desire.

'Is this what you really want, princess?' he groaned. 'Because if you don't, we'd better stop this right now.'

Her arms were still around his neck, their hips still intimately meshed. She could feel the growing power of him and realised how much he wanted her. And how much of an effort it must have taken for him to say that.

'Yes, I do,' she said almost shyly—which was crazy when she considered that she hadn't been in the least shy with him before. But that night and that capitulation had been motivated by passion, pure and sweet and undiluted. While this...

This was love—more potent than any other emotion in

the world. But only for *her*, she reminded herself. Only for her. Guy wasn't making any declarations—he was just a man, with a man's libido.

And maybe, knowing that, she should have stopped him, but Sabrina knew that no force in the world could have stopped her. Not when she wanted Guy this badly. 'Yes,' she said again. 'Yes.'

He found the gleam of flesh on her pale shoulder utterly irresistible and trickled a slow finger over its satin curve, watching as she shivered in response.

'Mmm,' he murmured, as he slipped first one strap down and then the other, so that the material fell in soft folds to her waist. Her tiny breasts were thrusting furiously against the soft lavender lace of her bra, the tips rosy and hard, and he nudged the pad of his thumb against one, seeing her body jerk automatically in response.

Her eyelids fluttered to a close. 'Guy!' She uttered his name in choked response to that first touch, feeling the wet, wild warmth of response.

'Feels good, doesn't it?' he murmured, circling his thumb with feather-light torment.

Good? It felt as if she'd just been catapulted straight into a place where nothing existed but pure sensation. 'It feels fantastic,' she moaned.

'No, *you* feel fantastic.' His closed his hand possessively over one tiny breast and her nails immediately dug into his neck as she swayed against him, communicating her heated reaction as clearly as if she'd spoken it.

Guy frowned. She was so damned responsive! He always took his women to bed. Always. And yet suddenly he discovered that he didn't want to break the spell by moving from where they were and taking their clothes off. He wanted to do it to her right here. And right now. It was as simple and as elemental as that.

'I don't know if I can make it to the bedroom,' he groaned.

'Who cares?' she whispered back.

'You mean you don't?'

'No.' She would swing from the chandelier if he wanted her to.

He pushed her down onto the carpet and joined her there, pulling her into his arms and kissing her while his hand slid beneath her dress and smoothed it all the way up to her thighs. He gazed down at their milky pale curves and felt his resolve slipping away. 'I don't know if I can even bear the time to take your clothes off, princess. Or mine.' He grazed her a light stroking touch where she was most responsive, smiling as her body bucked against his hand.

Sabrina's head fell back against the Persian carpet as she felt the first honeyed flutter of his fingers, and her thighs parted for him of their own volition. 'Then don't,' she breathed hoarsely, feeling as wanton right then as she had ever felt. 'Don't. Let's just do it.'

She found herself fumbling at the button of his trousers, then rasping the zip down with difficulty, her hand straying agitatedly over his hard swell, and she heard him suck in a ragged breath.

'Make that a definite,' he moaned as he tugged her panties down right over her thighs, skimming them impatiently over her ankles and then tossing them over his shoulder. 'Now, my little temptress…'

Hearing the slumberous intent in his voice, Sabrina opened her eyes to see him kick off his trousers, exposing the true, daunting power of his arousal, and she shivered as he came to kneel over her.

He bent his head and touched his mouth against hers as he positioned himself close to her. Tantalisingly close. 'Want me?' he whispered.

She couldn't think of a time when she hadn't. Not if she

was being honest with herself. 'Oh, God, yes,' she moaned helplessly, as she writhed her hips impatiently beneath his.

'Well, then…' And he groaned as he entered her with one single, powerful thrust. 'You've got me.'

This time was different. This time she knew him—or at least as much of him as he was prepared to let her know. For there was always some sense that Guy was holding something of himself back. But who cared? Maybe she would never have all of him—but no person could ever totally possess another, could they?

But now—physically at least—he was as abandoned as she had only ever dreamed he could be.

In Venice he had been a skilful lover, but they had been strangers. This time his kisses were deeper, his caresses more tender. With each long, deep stroke, she felt enchained by his possession. It *felt* different. As if it really mattered.

No. That was simply an illusion, she forced herself to remember. Just the body's way of tricking the mind into thinking that this was something more than just a basic human need. She tried to keep a hold on her sanity, even as the first waves of orgasm began to shimmer her down into its sweet, shuddering waters. And only sanity prevented her from crying out how much she loved him.

Guy watched the arching of her back and the indolent splaying of her limbs, and only when he saw her body begin to judder and bloom did he allow himself to let go, to the most exquisite release.

Afterwards they lay together on the carpet, dipping in and out of a slumberous doze, their limbs still damp and tangled.

He heard her yawn and looked to where her tousled red-blonde hair lay ribboned across his chest. 'You do realise,' he murmured sleepily, 'that we're still half-dressed?'

She looked down at herself. Then at him.

Her dress lay rucked up to her waist, while Guy was wearing nothing but a T-shirt. She could see the beautifully pale curves of his buttocks and she felt a warm heat begin to suffuse her.

'Oh.'

He rolled on to her and captured her face as his hips crushed hers beneath him. 'Is that all you can say—"Oh"?' He saw her squirm and her agitated look and his eyes narrowed. *'Oh,'* he repeated softly, but he managed to fill the word with a sultry promise. 'Maybe we *had* better go to bed.'

Sabrina swallowed. 'What, right now?'

He smiled. 'Mmm. Right now.' And he pulled her to her feet, shaking his head as he saw her look around the room for her underwear. 'Leave that,' he instructed softly. 'You won't be needing any clothes tonight.' And saw her shivered response.

He took her by the hand and led her to his bedroom, in a section of the large flat she usually avoided, throwing the door open to reveal an airy room dominated by an enormous bed. Huge windows looked down onto the flower-filled square.

'I don't think you've ever been in here before, have you, princess?' he murmured. 'Do you like it?'

'Well, I have seen it,' admitted Sabrina, and saw the question in his eyes. 'I sneaked a look when I first moved in. I was...curious.' More than curious.

She had wanted to see whether the room could tell her more about the man, but it had thrown up few clues. The paintings were superb, the furniture modern and luxurious—but it was an oddly dispassionate room. As though he was wary about expressing too much of his personality through mere fixtures and fittings. Again, there was that distinctive air of containment.

Guy should have been riled at what could definitely have

been termed as an intrusion, but found himself smiling instead. He thought that few people would have admitted it. But then wasn't Sabrina's innate innocence one of her sweetest and most appealing features? Well, that and her stubborn insistence and the way she could make him mad and then make him smile an instant later. Even the way she nagged him about working too hard—which his mother had long given up on.

'Do you mind?' she asked. 'That I sneaked a look?'

He saw the uncertainty which had clouded the ice-blue eyes, and a wave of an emotion he didn't recognise washed over him. He forced himself instead to watch the pert thrust of her breasts.

'I'm rather turned on by the thought of you prowling around in here like a pussy-cat,' he said roughly. 'Come on, let's go to bed.'

## CHAPTER FOURTEEN

SABRINA opened her eyes to the morning light and closed them again as images of the previous night came flickering back.

What had she *done*? Placed herself in the most precariously vulnerable position in the world—that was what she'd done. Given herself to Guy, heart, body and soul.

'Good morning, princess,' came a murmured greeting, and her eyes snapped open to see Guy standing, towering above her, already shaved and dressed for work in another exquisitely cut dark suit, and she felt a great wrench of longing.

'Hello,' she whispered, her heart thundering at the sight of him.

He smiled. 'You were sleeping so beautifully that I couldn't bear to wake you.'

She sat up and saw his eyes darken as her bare breasts were exposed, and some protective instinct made her gather the sheet around her.

'You're going already?' she asked him.

'Wish I didn't have to, but I have an early meeting,' he said softly, and sat down on the bed beside her.

Of course he did. Guy the workaholic. Guy the driven. He might have spent most of the night making exquisite love to her, but that didn't change his priorities, did it? And work came first. It always would.

Well, she might have been compliant in his arms last night, but that didn't mean that she had to exist in a passive state of insecurity now.

'This changes things, doesn't it?' she said slowly.

There was an imperceptible pause as the grey eyes narrowed. He'd hoped to avoid any kind of analysis. 'How come?'

'Oh, don't be obtuse, Guy, you're much too intelligent for that,' she told him crossly. 'If I'm living with you...' She saw the wariness on his face and wished she'd phrased it better. 'If I'm living here and we're having—'

'Sex?' he put in, with a wicked grin.

Thank goodness he'd interrupted her. She'd been about to say 'a relationship', but his drawled one-word question had brought what had just happened between them down to the lowest common denominator. And shown her more clearly than anything else could have done just how different their agendas were. She might love Guy—but that didn't mean he felt the same way about her. Men didn't need to be *in* love to make love the way he had done.

'Yes, sex.' She swallowed.

'Good sex.' He trickled a finger slowly from shoulder to breast, and she let the sheet fall. 'The very best,' he added slowly.

It should have been a compliment, so why did it sound little short of an insult? 'Thank you,' she said stiffly.

He flicked softly at one rosy nipple, feeling it surge into instant life beneath his finger. God, he felt like just getting back into bed with her and forgetting the damned meeting. His face hardened. He hadn't got where he was today by letting a woman trap him with her honeyed sweetness.

'Why should it change anything, except for the better?' he questioned softly. 'We carry on as we were, only now you share my bed at night. I can't think of anything I'd rather have.'

'No,' she said sadly. Of course he couldn't. He didn't want commitment, or even a relationship. He wanted sex, pure and simple—and obviously he thought that was all she wanted, too. And who could blame him? Hadn't she always demonstrated the sensual side of her nature around him?

He reluctantly moved his hand from her breast and cupped her face instead. 'What's the problem, Sabrina?' he asked gently. 'Why the long face? Let's just enjoy it, huh?'

And when she came to the end of her stay with him, what then? But consenting adults didn't make unnecessary emotional demands, did they? Guy didn't love *her*—and wouldn't he doubt *her* feelings if he had any idea what they were? Wouldn't he consider her fickle if she told him she'd fallen in love with him—only months after the death of the man she'd been due to spend the rest of her life with?

But love could strike without warning. It wasn't exclusive. Just because she'd been in love once before, that didn't mean it couldn't happen again. What she'd felt for Michael hadn't been what she felt for Guy. Her feelings were different, but that didn't make them any less valid. And they were all-consuming.

She wanted him, she realised, on whatever terms he was prepared to take her.

But he wouldn't know that. She would keep her dignity and play at being a modern woman, not a lovesick fool who would settle for anything—just as long as it included him.

'OK, let's just enjoy it,' she echoed, and slanted him a smile.

Her look was one of pure provocation, and just for one second Guy wavered, itching to undress and climb into bed with her and lose himself in her body.

But he'd broken so many rules where Sabrina was concerned—wouldn't one more be his downfall? Hadn't he controlled his life according to a rigid plan laid down by the circumstances of his youth? It would be nothing short of recklessness to go in deeper than he already was. Her fiancé wasn't long gone, he reminded himself. For Sabrina, this was a purely physical affair on the rebound. It had to be. Logic told him that.

He stood up quickly, not trusting himself to kiss her. Just being this close to her and knowing she was stark naked underneath that sheet was playing havoc with his senses. 'Time I was out of here,' he said abruptly, and then softened to give her a smile. 'I'll see you tonight, princess.'

She watched him go, heard the front door slam, shatteringly aware that he hadn't even kissed her. Maybe she should be grateful for that. At least he wasn't filling her head with false promises of happy-ever-after.

She sighed. They would carry on as before. Living together—only this time, as Guy had so unromantically put it, with sex as part of the equation.

The next three weeks ticked away like a time-bomb, with Sabrina alternating between giddy elation and wild despair but determined to show neither emotion.

Guy took her to the theatre, and to concerts. He even skipped work on the Saturdays when she was off and they explored London together, like tourists.

And at night…

At night he couldn't seem to keep his hands off her. And it was really quite disturbing how one dark, sensual look levelled mockingly at her across the sitting room was enough to send her running straight into his arms.

While sometimes she despised herself for her instant surrender whenever he touched her, at least she had the comfort of knowing that it didn't seem any different for him. She could reduce him to putty in her hands.

Why, she had even made him late for work this morning, and thrown his careful schedule into disarray. All because she had strolled into the bathroom one morning, wearing nothing but a pair of silver camiknickers while he'd been combing his hair.

Guy had stilled as he'd seen her reflection in the mirror, the pale swell of her breasts and the long curve of her legs beneath the frivolous lace trim. A pulse had begun to beat steadily at his temple.

'What are you doing?' he asked, in an odd kind of voice.

She batted him an innocent smile as she bent down to retrieve a book from where she'd been reading it in the bath the previous night while waiting for him to get back from Rome.

'I forgot this,' she said, and straightened up.

But the sight of the silver silk stretching tightly over her bottom had been enough to send his senses into overdrive. He put the comb down with a hand which wasn't quite steady.

'Kiss me goodbye,' he ordered throatily.

She went into his arms without a word, and pressed her lips to his, feeling them part on a sigh to greet her. 'Goodbye,' she whispered, but she couldn't resist moving her body closer and feeling the sudden responding tension in his.

His hand snaked around her waist, drawing her in closer still. He was painfully and erotically aware of her barely clothed state, even through the thickness of the suit he wore.

Trapped against his hard, virile body, Sabrina felt the warm pooling of a desire so strong that she couldn't have resisted it if she had tried. And she certainly wasn't trying.

'I don't want to be late,' he ground out, but once again he drove his mouth down onto hers in a sweet, crushing kiss.

'God forbid,' she murmured, and flicked her tongue inside his mouth, hearing him groan in response.

'Stop it, Sabrina,' he pleaded, but only half-heartedly.

Caught up with longing and compelled by a need to shatter that rigid control, she moulded her breasts brazenly against his torso. 'Stop what?' she murmured, and allowed her fingers to trickle down over the rocky shaft of his erection, feeling him jerk in distracted response. 'Do you want me to stop this?' She ran her hand expertly over him. 'Do you, Guy?'

A shudder ran through him as he felt her begin to unzip him. There would be no stopping now, he realised with a hot, heady rush of blood, and then his hands were on her breasts, feeling them spring into excited life beneath his hungry fingertips.

She struggled to free the zip and the trousers fell redundantly to his ankles. She heard him swear softly, and then, very deliberately, he moved the damp silk panel of her camiknickers aside and delved his fingers deep into the honeyed moistness. She gasped.

'Do you like that?' he murmured, feeling her thighs instantly parting for him. 'Do you?'

Her response was instant and overwhelming. Sabrina swayed as she clasped his dark head against her, murmuring a protest she didn't feel, her knees sagging weakly as she felt the swift heat of need. He lifted his head to glitter her a look of provocative assessment and swiftly turned her over so that she was bending over the bath.

He ripped her camiknickers off without compunction and let his silk boxer shorts fall to his ankles, and she realised that he was going to...going to...

'Oh, Guy!' she gasped ecstatically, as he entered her.

He groaned as he submerged himself in her hot, molten depths, thinking that it shouldn't be this simple—or this out of control. And then he wasn't doing any thinking at all. The world had shifted focus and then hardened, to a brighter focus, and now it splintered out of all recognition as they both cried out at the same time.

He pulled out of her and turned her around, thinking how shaken she looked. Well, hell, he was pretty shaken himself. When had he ever acted like *that* before? In Venice, he reminded himself grimly, that was when.

'You've made me late for work,' was all he said. Then he gave her a hard, crushing kiss before turning and swiftly walking out of the bathroom.

Flushed with orgasm, and a bitter kind of regret, Sabrina slammed the lock home behind him and then sank to her knees on the bathroom floor as dry, shuddering sobs began to tear at her throat. What on earth was happening to them?

As a demonstration of lust, that experience had been in a class of its own. Guy had used her for sex, but hadn't she gone ahead and *allowed* herself to be used? She loved him, yes, but he'd never given any indication that he felt even a *fraction* of love for her. And she didn't want to love again. Not like this. Bad enough that she'd loved and lost Michael—but at least Michael had felt the same way about *her*.

And she had known then with a sinking certainty that this one-sided love would bring her nothing but heartbreak. Far better to begin to distance herself. Starting from now.

It was late-night shopping this evening, and she'd make herself go browsing round after she'd finished work, deliberately make herself late home.

But Guy was even later. He'd had to juggle his day to include the missed meeting, and then had sat through it, bored and distracted, trying not to keep glancing down at his watch and thinking about Sabrina.

This was getting slightly ridiculous, he thought exasperatedly as he let himself into the flat. Going home at night had become the highlight of his day.

But tonight there was no meal cooking.

Just Sabrina sitting on the sofa, looking moody, an unopened book lying on her lap.

He dropped his briefcase and gave her a thoughtful look. 'Hi,' he said softly.

'Hi.'

He thought how wooden her voice sounded. And maybe he deserved it. 'Sabrina, listen—about this morning—'

'No, Guy, please.' She shook her head, her cheeks growing pink as shame vied with remembered pleasure. 'It happened—let's forget it.'

That was the trouble—he couldn't forget it. It had been on his mind all day. And so had she. 'I shouldn't have been so abrupt with you afterwards.'

'No, you shouldn't!' She threw him a furious look. 'And maybe *I* shouldn't have committed the terrible sin of wandering in looking like that when you were getting ready for work. How wicked of me to unwittingly throw temptation in your path, Guy! Heaven forbid that you should ever break your rigid routine and be *late*!'

'Sabrina,' he said softly, 'are we going to fight about this all night?'

'No, we aren't.' She drew a deep breath. They weren't going to fight about anything and she was going to be very calm and grown-up about what she had to say. 'We ought to talk about me going.'

He went very still, as though he hadn't heard her properly. '*Going?*' he echoed. 'What are you talking about?' His voice softened. 'Aren't you taking things a little too far, princess? I know what we did was pretty wham-bam-and-thank-you-ma'am, but there's no need to overreact.'

'This has nothing to do with this morning.' But she forced herself to remember that brutal and loveless kiss, and that somehow made what she had to say all the easier. 'I only came here on a temporary basis, remember? And the six weeks are nearly up.'

If she'd detonated a small bomb on the carpet in front of him he couldn't have been more shell-shocked. Her stay had merged into one pleasurable and sensual blur. Had she really been here for *that* long? Guy stared at her. 'But you aren't really going?'

It was a million miles away from the 'please, don't go' she'd been hopelessly praying for. She kept her face carefully composed. 'I have to, Guy—I won't have a job after next Friday, and they won't hold my job in Salisbury. Believe it or not, jobs in bookshops are highly sought-after.'

He could believe it quite easily—but then he'd seen her at work. A meeting had been cancelled and he'd called for her unexpectedly one lunchtime, dismissively waving away her protests that she'd brought a sandwich with her.

'We'll feed it to the pigeons,' he'd murmured, thinking that the books and the old polished wood of the shop only seemed to enhance her bright-haired beauty. One look at Sabrina sitting busy at her desk, and any sane person would have thought it the most perfect job in the world.

'So leave.' He shrugged.

Sabrina froze. 'Leave?'

Guy gave a slow smile. 'Sure. I can support you.'

'I don't want your support,' she said stiffly. 'Or your charity.'

'Sabrina.' His voice softened as he walked across the room and sat down beside her on the sofa, not missing the almost imperceptible shift of her body as she leaned away from him. 'It's not charity. I earn obscene amounts of money—'

'You said it, Guy.'

His eyes narrowed. 'You don't *need* to work,' he said quietly.

'*I don't need to work?*' she repeated in disbelief, before leaping to her feet to stare down at him in an angry blaze. 'Says who? Says *you*! Well, if that's the case, you don't know anything, Guy, not really!'

'Oh? This is fast becoming a real home-truth session,' he drawled. 'Do continue, Sabrina—I'm fascinated.'

'Don't you have any idea about my need for independence?' she stormed, ignoring the dangerous note in his voice. 'Or did you think I would just fall to the ground in a grateful heap because you've offered to "support" me?'

'Clearly not,' came the dry retort. A lot of women would have done. His mother, for example, had never forgotten what he'd done for her. But that had been different. That had been called survival.

Jenna, he realised, would have adored the idea. So would many of the other trust-fund babes. Not Sabrina, though, he realised slowly. Her principles were in a different class.

'It's *your* flat!' she stormed. '*You* have all the control here—so just imagine if you started paying for me, too. How unequal would *that* make things? At least buying groceries now and then makes me feel as though I'm doing my bit!'

He looked at her steadily. 'So what do you suggest we do?'

She looked at him sadly, realising that she'd talked herself into a corner. There was no solution—or at least not one that would make her happy. Only one thing could do that, and he wasn't offering her permanence.

Because if she accepted his offer to stay while he supported her, then where would that leave her? Busy clinging on to a relationship which would grow increasingly more one-sided.

Even if she found herself another job here in London, wouldn't that just be postponing the inevitable heartbreak when he tired of her?

'I'll leave at the end of next week,' she said impassively. 'As orginally planned.'

Guy's body quickened, even as his heart felt the unfamiliar pang of rejection. But if she was expecting him to *beg* her to change her mind, she had a lot to learn about him. Needing something enough to beg made you vulnerable, and he had once made a vow never to be vulnerable again. He paused. 'So, until you go, will we continue as...before, Sabrina?'

How very delicately phrased, she thought with a slight tinge of hysteria. 'You mean, will I be sharing your bed at night?'

He thought that there were a few more flattering ways she could have described it. 'That's exactly what I mean,' he answered coolly.

Her hunger for him warred with her self-respect, but it was never going to be much of a battle. She thought about how bleak her future would be without him, and knew that she wanted to savour every last, glorious moment. 'Ask me tonight,' she said flippantly.

He knew from the darkening of her eyes just what her answer would be, but any triumph was eclipsed by a slow, ticking anger. So she thought she could just play cat and mouse with him when it suited her, did she?

He rose to his feet with stealthy grace and pulled her into his arms without warning. 'Why don't I ask you now?' he drawled, before claiming her mouth in a kiss which had her reeling.

## CHAPTER FIFTEEN

SABRINA let herself into the flat with a heavy heart and went to put the shopping in the kitchen.

Two more days. Just two.

It was inconceivable. Especially as Guy had spent the last few days seemingly hell-bent on showing her just what she would be missing. He didn't seem satisfied until he had her sobbing out her shuddering pleasure, night after night...but he'd never asked her to stay.

She made herself a coffee and then went to stand at the window, where the bright hues of early summer dazzled from the garden in the square. How on earth could she ever go back to being what she had been?

Or maybe that was the wrong way to look at it. She could never really go back to being the old Sabrina—there was a new one now, ready and willing to take her place. And rebirth, like birth, was always painful. Why else would she feel this terrible, tearing pain at the thought of never seeing Guy Masters again?

Would he miss her? she wondered achingly. Probably, just a little, yes. And certainly in bed. But the missing, like their relationship, would be unequal. Guy called the shots and Guy had all the control. He would miss her for a little while and then move on.

Sabrina glanced down at her watch. It was only just past six, so there was at least an hour and a half before he would grace the flat with his presence.

She had bought a load of cheap vegetables at the market, and she had just begun to chop them in order to make a soup when there was a sharp ring at the doorbell. Wiping her hands down over the apron which she insisted on wearing, and which Guy always teased her about, Sabrina went to answer it, to find Tom Roberts standing on the doorstep.

'Hi, Tom.' She smiled affectionately.

She'd last seen Guy's cousin at a drinks party a couple of weeks ago, and then he'd been sipping at a Bloody Mary and laughing at something Sabrina had said. But today he looked wary.

'Hi, Sabrina—may I come in?'

'Oh, yes, of course, of course,' babbled Sabrina, and pulled the door open. 'Only I'm afraid that Guy isn't back from work yet.'

'I know that. It isn't Guy I've come to see. It's you.'

'Oh.' She smiled. 'That's nice. You'd better come in.'

'Thanks.' He followed her into the sitting room and sat down.

Sabrina looked at him expectantly. 'Can I get you a drink, Tom?'

'No, thanks—I'm out to dinner later and Trudi will kill me if I turn up with an inane grin on my face.' He suddenly grew serious. 'Is it really true? Guy says you're leaving.'

Hearing the words spoken aloud like that by a third person made Sabrina realise just how horribly true it was.

'That's right. I am.'

'But, Sabrina, why? I mean, I've never seen him looking so contented—happy, even! And you're the first woman he's ever lived with, even though women have been mounting campaigns to snare him for years. He says that he doesn't want you to go, but that you're going anyway. So why?'

She shook her head. 'I can't go into it, Tom. It's too complicated, and it isn't fair on Guy.'

'Fair on Guy?' Tom repeated slowly. 'Sabrina, look…' He seemed to be having difficulty choosing the right words.

'I've known Guy all my life, but, with him, what you see isn't automatically what you get.'

'You're talking in riddles, Tom.'

He pulled a face. 'Everyone looks at him and thinks that he's Mr Invulnerable—strong and rich and powerful—'

'Maybe that's because he *is*,' observed Sabrina drily.

'Yeah, I know all that. And that's what he likes to project. But that's only part of the package—he keeps a lot of himself hidden. That highly controlled and tough exterior he's cultivated—that's what he shows to the world.'

'You're telling me,' said Sabrina bitterly. 'The man for whom the term, "workaholic" was invented.'

'And have you never stopped to ask yourself why?'

'Tom, you know him better than almost anyone—so you must also know that he doesn't like to talk about himself.'

'Well, maybe it's about time you tried! I mean, like, *really* tried! Have you?'

'When a door is kept locked you give up trying to open it,' she said.

'You could always try kicking it down,' he suggested softly.

'Women don't kick doors down,' Sabrina objected, forgetting for a moment that they were talking metaphorically.

'But they can,' he objected. 'It just takes longer.'

She stared at Tom, taken aback by his vehemence, even though that wary look was still in place on his face. There was, she realised, something he wasn't telling her. And she knew that his loyalty to his cousin meant he wouldn't disclose it. 'Maybe I should,' she agreed slowly.

'Anyway...' Tom rose to his feet. 'Time I was going. And there's no need to mention to Guy that I was here.'

She shook her head. 'Don't worry. I won't.'

After he'd gone, Sabrina prowled the flat, the soup forgotten, and realised that she'd been guilty of some sort of emotional cowardice. She'd fought for her independence, and a kind of equality with Guy, and yet she'd allowed herself to be daunted by that enigmatic, don't-ask-me quality of his.

She had shared his life, and his bed, but had stood on the sidelines when it had come to exploring his feelings—mainly out of a selfish sense of self-preservation. She'd known that he hadn't wanted her to ask, and so she hadn't. She'd wanted Guy, but hadn't been prepared to risk being hurt by him—and you couldn't do that in a relationship. Loving someone automatically made you vulnerable to pain.

I've got to talk to him, she told herself. Whatever happens, I can't leave him without having done that.

Guy cut his meeting short, and it was clear from his secretary's expression that she clearly thought he had taken leave of his senses.

Well, maybe he had.

Or maybe he was just coming to his senses.

He found himself asking why he was prepared to let someone like Sabrina simply walk out of his life without argument. As if he had no control over the future. As though, because of one long-ago act, a pattern had been set in his life and he was powerless to change it. It was ironic, really, that he—the master of control—was allowing events to gather up speed by themselves.

He'd spent his life shielding himself from the prying questions of women on the make. Yet Sabrina was clearly *not* on the make—and neither did she ask him questions.

He was so caught up in his thoughts that he missed his stop on the tube. Another first, he thought wryly as he walked home in the golden summer sunshine. But the idea that Guy Masters—the cool and controlled Guy Masters—had misjudged a train journey he'd been making for the past who-knew-how-many years actually had him smiling ruefully.

He walked into the flat. 'Sabrina?' He watched while she drifted out of the sitting room, as graceful as that water nymph he'd first compared her to in Venice.

'Hello,' she said softly.

She'd used her waiting hour to shower, and to change and carefully apply her make-up. Because this was important, she realised. Very important. And, like a job interview she was determined to win, she just wanted to look her best. It was as simple as that.

Guy wanted to kiss her. Hell, he wanted to lose himself in the sweet torment of her body. But he didn't trust himself to touch her. Sometimes desire could cloud judgement, and right then he needed every bit of judgement he'd ever possessed.

'I need to talk to you, Sabrina.'

'And I need to talk to you.'

He nodded, but absently, as if he'd scarcely heard her. Like a man with a lot on his mind.

'Let's go into the sitting room,' he said abruptly.

Sabrina nodded as she followed him, vaguely disappointed at something in his tone but determined not to lose her nerve. She would chip, chip, chip away until she found out what she needed to know and what Tom hadn't been able to tell her.

In the sitting room neither of them sat, but instead stood looking at each other warily, like two fighters sizing each other up before a duel.

'Do you want to leave?' he demanded. 'I mean, really?'

Truth? Or lie? Communication? Or hiding behind social niceties? What did she have to lose? 'Of course I don't!'

Relief flooded his veins like a drug, and Guy drew in a deep breath. 'Well, that's good—because I don't want you to either. I want you to stay here. With me.'

Sabrina stared at him steadily. She had played her part—now she needed to know the truth from *him*. 'Why?'

How else to say this without shooting straight from the hip? But Guy used words carefully—he recognised their power and their significance—and there were certain words that he would not use lightly. Or recklessly. Unless he was certain that he meant them. And he didn't want to frighten her either. Or push her into something before she was ready. 'I…care for you, Sabrina,' he said slowly. 'That's why.'

So he cared for her. It was a curiously colourless way to phrase it, but Sabrina nodded her head slowly, less disappointed than she'd imagined she would be. He wasn't offering her the moon, no, but it was a start. For Guy to even *admit* caring for her was something. Because he was not, she knew, a man who would make a declaration without thinking it through first, or without meaning it.

But if she stayed then there had to be a new honesty between them. 'Why leave it until the day before I was going?' she demanded. 'Why on earth didn't you say something before?'

'Because I was burying my head in the sand and believing in the impossible.' He sighed. 'I imagined that my life would continue in its calm and uncluttered way once you'd gone. I didn't realise that the thought of you not being here was going to drive me out of my mind!'

Well, that was a bit better. A lot better. She actually smiled, but the smile had a hint of reproof about it. 'Hell, Guy, I've virtually packed all my suitcases!'

'Then unpack them,' he drawled silkily, but something in her face made him backtrack. He owed her more than that rather dispassionate request that she stay with him. 'Listen to me, Sabrina. I'm no good at trust—you'll have to help me. I'm used to women who are…' he paused '…*different* from you.'

Women who wouldn't want to know him if he was just an average guy. Not like Sabrina. She'd fallen under his spell without knowing *who* he was. His gaze was unflickering. 'And I guess my childhood sowed the seeds of distrust almost from the start.'

She held her breath. Here, she was certain, lay the key to the barrier he'd erected around himself. This was what Tom had been hinting at. 'Do you want to tell me about it?' she asked him softly.

He paused only for as long as it took to be mesmerised by the ice-blue dazzle of her eyes. 'Yes,' he said simply, and gave a long sigh. 'You're always complaining that I work too hard…'

Her persistence had, in fact, sown the first seeds of doubt in his mind. Had made him look closely at her accusations. 'And you've made me see how right you are. When you live alone, there's no one to question you—no one to compare yourself with. It's become a habit that's hard to break, a habit that started a long time ago…'

'Tell me, Guy,' she urged quietly, remembering how he'd let her unburden herself over Michael. And suspecting that he now needed to do the same for himself.

His mouth flattened. 'My father was the opposite to the way I am—his whole life was a reckless gamble. He would hear about some sure-fire scheme to make money and he would invest everything he had. Our life became a lottery. My mother and my brother and I used to find ourselves living in mansions. Or hovels, more often than not,' he went on, with a disparaging shrug. 'With my mother trying to feed two growing boys—and next to nothing in the cupboard. I guess it was just fortunate that a family trust paid for our education, or things would have come to a head much sooner.'

'But something happened?' prompted Sabrina, hurting

herself at the look of pain which had frozen his features. 'Something really bad?'

Was it that obvious? he wondered. He'd thought that he'd trained his face to hide all emotion—but Sabrina seemed to have the ability to make it come creeping back again. The words he'd locked away for so long came tumbling out as if they couldn't wait to be spoken.

'His schemes became more and more bizarre and my mother grew concerned. She tried to get all our assets put in her name, but he was far cleverer than she was. I guess these days she wouldn't have stayed with him—but things were different then. And she was loyal, too.' Just as you would be, he thought suddenly.

He saw her look of horror and heard himself defending his father. And that was something else he'd only just realised. That, whatever wrong he had done, his father was still his father.

'Oh, it wasn't a malicious action on his part—more a lack of judgement and a sense of misplaced pride. But one day he went too far and lost everything.' Guy shrugged. 'The business, the house, the car. Everything. With debts galore thrown in for good measure. Only this time his spirit was broken, too. I was fifteen, and my brother was twelve.'

There was a grim silence. Sabrina didn't say a word.

'My mother's parents took us in—they had a beautiful big house close to the cliffs in Cornwall.' His eyes grew distant as he thought back to a time he'd buried away deep in the recesses of his mind. 'But accepting charity—even family charity—was anathema to my father. He tried working in paid employment, but he could never cope with working for other people. His mood went down and there seemed to be no way that anyone could reach out and help him. And he and my mother never communicated particularly well.'

Sabrina nodded. That explained a lot, too. Guy's fear of

relationships, his wariness of commitment and sharing. A bad role-model could put you off for life.

His face grew dark as he forced himself to say the words. 'One night he went out and never came back again.'

'What happened?' whispered Sabrina hoarsely.

He didn't coat it with any sugar. 'He went out walking on the cliff-top. It was a wild night and the wind was blowing up a storm. He fell… We'll never know what really happened—whether he lost his footing, or if the wind caught him off balance. Or whether he jumped.'

He met her eyes with such a bleak expression that Sabrina couldn't help herself. In fact, even if he'd been just about to kick her out she still would have gone straight over and put her arms around him and hugged him as tightly as she knew how. Trying, however futilely, to take some of his pain away.

'Oh, Guy,' she whispered brokenly. 'Guy.'

He dropped a kiss onto her beautiful head, but forced himself to continue, feeling the burden lifting even as he shared it with her.

'I determined then that I would never be placed in such a vulnerable position again—and neither would my mother or brother.'

'So how did you manage?'

'Against everyone's advice, I left school at sixteen and started working, and I never really stopped. Khalim's father gave me a break, and I was off.' Off on a merry-go-round of hard work which had continued until this bright-haired temptress had walked into his life.

Sabrina rubbed her cheek against his shirt. He'd told her everything she'd wanted to know, without her having to ask him. He'd trusted her enough to open up to her. Would his trust now spread out and out, like ripples on a pond, so that their relationship got bigger and bigger?

'I didn't plan to feel this way about you, Sabrina,' he

admitted huskily as he caught her by the shoulders and forced her to look up at him, his own eyes soft with promise.

She felt the glimmer of tears. 'As if anyone has any control over their feelings.' She gulped. 'I wasn't planning on…' Her words tailed off. To talk of love would frighten him almost as much as it frightened her.

'On what?'

'Needing you like this,' she compromised.

'Need can be a powerful emotion, princess.' He tipped her chin upwards with the tip of his finger and gave a slightly shell-shocked smile. 'I find I need *you* pretty badly myself.'

She recognised what it had cost him to admit that. She stood on tiptoe to plant a soft kiss on his lips, and he sighed.

'So you'll stay?' he asked.

She drew her mouth away, her dreamy expression replaced by one of caution. Should she stay? But did she really have any alternative, when the thought of leaving filled her with a kind of mad despair?

All he'd told her was that he cared for her. He'd made no promise other than an unspoken one, which was that he trusted her enough to open up his heart. And surely trust— coming from a man like Guy—was worth all the most passionate declarations in the world.

'Sabrina?' he prompted softly.

'You know I will.'

'What's the date?' he asked suddenly, stroking a red-gold lock of hair off her cheek.

She thought back to all the order forms she'd filled in at the bookshop that morning. 'June the tenth. Why?'

He kissed the tip of her nose. 'Just remember it,' he urged softly.

# EPILOGUE

GUY closed the front door and turned to look at Sabrina, a slow smile lighting up his face as he thought how beautiful she looked in her mint-green dress with her glorious bright hair tied back with a matching green ribbon.

'So, how did that go, do you think?' he asked her.

'I think they enjoyed it.' Her eyes glinted with mischief. 'Your mother kept asking me whether we'd arranged a wedding date.'

'And what did you say?'

'I said no, of course. Because we haven't.' But there was no resentment in her voice. 'And your sister-in-law kept telling me how much she had enjoyed her two pregnancies.'

'I'll bet she did!' He grinned. 'Like some more champagne?'

She'd barely touched a drop all afternoon. She'd been so nervous about meeting Guy's mother and stepfather and his brother and wife and their two children. But the lunch had gone like a dream, and now relief began to seep into her veins. 'Love some.'

He opened up the French doors leading onto the balcony and brought out two fizzing flutes. He handed her one as they sat side by side on the small bench, turning their faces towards the sun.

'Do you know what the date is, princess?' he asked quietly.

The glass was halfway to her mouth, but she quickly put it down on the decking and turned to look at him as a distant memory stirred in her mind. 'But you know the date!' she exclaimed. 'We've had this lunch in the diary for ages. It's June the tenth. Why?'

He put his own glass down to join hers—champagne was the very last thing on his mind. 'It's exactly a year since I persuaded you to stay,' he said softly. 'Remember?'

She nodded, mesmerised by the dawning tenderness on his face. 'I didn't take a lot of persuading,' she said drily.

He smiled. 'It didn't seem like that at the time. I knew then that I loved you, princess.' He lifted her hand to his mouth and kissed one fingertip after another. 'But I didn't want to rush you, or push you into something you weren't ready for. You needed time to recover from Michael's death and time to decide whether you could ever trust yourself to love again.'

'Oh, Guy,' she whispered, shaken by the depth of his understanding. 'Darling, darling Guy.'

'I love you,' he said in a wondering kind of tone, as though he had just discovered a foreign language in which he was fluent.

And Sabrina realised that deep in her heart she'd known that he loved her. Loving wasn't just about saying three little words—Guy had shown her in every way that counted that he cared. His consideration, his softness, his intelligent regard and respect for her and the beautiful power of his lovemaking had left her in no doubt of that whatsoever.

'I love you,' she said softly.

He leaned forward to gently kiss her. He had known that, too. Her love for him was as bright as the June sunshine which was beating down so warmly on their faces.

Their lives together had merged and harmonised. Guy had stopped working on Saturdays, too. And now he came home at a decent hour in the evenings—sometimes even before her—which was a good thing. Unwilling to lose her, Wells had created a new job for her—enlarging the children's section of the bookshop. Sabrina had organised author signings and related talks, which had been avidly and ecstatically received, and now she had groups of school-children from all over London to enjoy them.

'So will you marry me?' he asked, very, very softly. 'Now that you've had time to heal properly?

'Oh, yes, I'll marry you,' she responded huskily. 'You know I will.'

Sabrina looked at his dear, sweet face and her heart turned over with love for him. It was true that time was a great healer, but in a way Guy had been helping to heal her from the moment she'd met him. Some people didn't believe in love at first sight, but Sabrina did. Something primitive had shimmered down on them from the first moment they'd set eyes on each other, and since then the feeling had just grown and grown.

Some things happened because they were meant to, and she and Guy were meant to. You could call it fate or you could call it destiny, but Sabrina called it pure and perfect love.

We're delighted to announce that

*A Mediterranean Marriage*

is taking place in

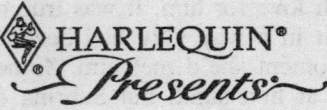

HARLEQUIN®
*Presents*

**This month, in THE BELLINI BRIDE by Michelle Reid, #2224**

Marco Bellini has to choose a suitable wife.
Will he make an honest woman of his
beautiful mistress, Antonia?

**In March you are invited to the wedding of
Rio Lombardi and Holly Samson
in THE ITALIAN'S WIFE by Lynne Graham, #2235**

When Holly, a homeless young woman, collapses in front of
Rio Lombardi's limousine, he feels compelled to take her and
her baby son home with him. Holly can't believe it when Rio
lavishes her with food, clothes…and a wedding ring….

*Harlequin Presents®*
The world's bestselling romance series.
Seduction and passion guaranteed!

*Available wherever Harlequin books are sold.*

HARLEQUIN®
*Makes any time special* ®

Visit us at www.eHarlequin.com

HPJANMM

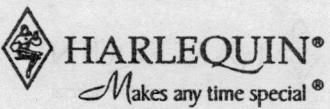

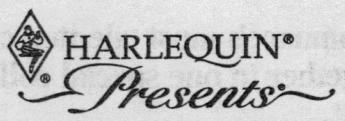

# HARLEQUIN®
## Presents~

**The world's bestselling romance series.**

Pick up a Harlequin Presents® novel and you will enter a world of spine-tingling passion and provocative, tantalizing romance!

2002 offers an exciting selection of titles by all your favorite authors.

**Are you looking for…?**

*Cole Cameron's Revenge*
#2223, January
by Sandra Marton

A Mediterranean Marriage

*The Bellini Bride* #2224, January
by Michelle Reid
*The Italian's Wife* #2235, March
by Lynne Graham

## Passion™

*His Miracle Baby* #2232, February
by Kate Walker
*A Secret Vengeance* #2236, March
by Miranda Lee
*The Secret Love Child* #2242, April
by Miranda Lee

MISTRESS TO A MILLIONAIRE

*The Billionaire Affair* #2238, March
by Diana Hamilton

LONDON'S MOST
ELIGIBLE PLAYBOYS

by Sharon Kendrick
*The Unlikely Mistress* #2227, January
*Surrender to the Sheikh*
#2233, February
*The Mistress's Child* #2239, March

**Seduction and
passion guaranteed!**

*Available wherever
Harlequin books are sold.*

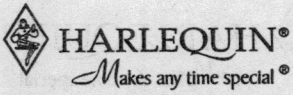
# HARLEQUIN®
*Makes any time special* ®

Visit us at www.eHarlequin.com

HPIBCGENP

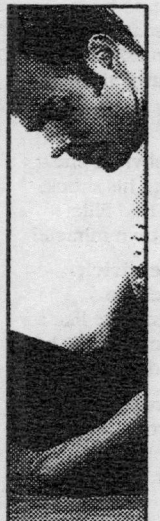
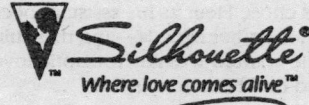

# Coming Next Month

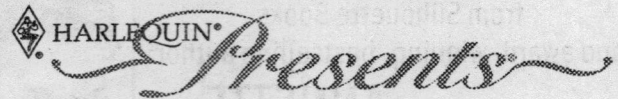

## THE BEST HAS JUST GOTTEN BETTER!

### #2229 THE CITY-GIRL BRIDE Penny Jordan
When elegant city girl Maggie Russell is caught in a country flood, rugged Finn Gordon comes to her rescue. He takes her to his farmhouse, laughs at her impractical designer clothes—and then removes them…piece by piece….

### #2230 A RICH MAN'S TOUCH Anne Mather
The arrival of businessman Gabriel Webb in Rachel's life is about to change everything! She isn't prepared when he touches emotions in her that she has carefully hidden away. But is Gabriel interested in only a fleeting affair?

### #2231 THE PROSPECTIVE WIFE Kim Lawrence
Matt's family are constantly trying to find him a wife, so he is instantly suspicious of blond, beautiful Kat. She's just as horrified to be suspected of being a prospective wife, but soon the talk of bedding and wedding starts to sound dangerously attractive—to both of them….

### #2232 HIS MIRACLE BABY Kate Walker
Morgan didn't know why Ellie had left him. It was obvious she'd still been in love with him. But when he found her, to his shock, she had the most adorable baby girl he'd ever seen. Had Ellie found another man or was this baby Morgan's very own miracle?

### #2233 SURRENDER TO THE SHEIKH Sharon Kendrick
The last thing Rose expected was to go on assignment to Prince Khalim's kingdom of Maraban. He treated her more like a princess than an employee. Rose knew she could never really be his princess—but their need for each other was so demanding….

### #2234 BY MARRIAGE DIVIDED Lindsay Armstrong
Bryn Wallis chose Fleur as his assistant because marriage was definitely not on her agenda—and that suited him perfectly. The last thing he wanted was any romantic involvement. Only, soon he began to find Fleur irresistible….